杨宪益 杨苡
兄妹译诗

杨宪益 杨苡 译著

赵蘅 绘

中国出版集团
中译出版社

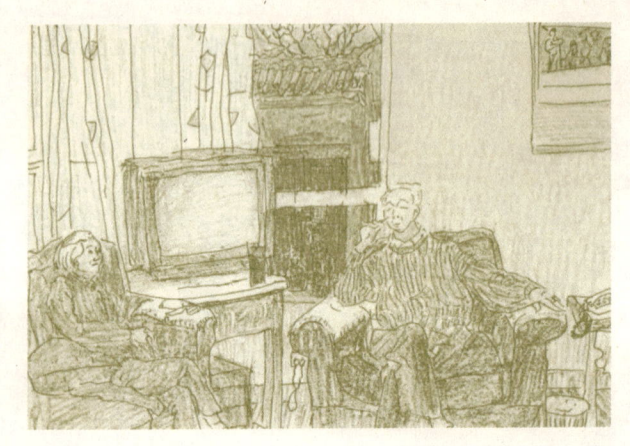

杨苡和杨宪益 赵蘅／绘

目录

辑一

在我随意游荡的每条路上，与我一同走，向同一的方向，有那幽美而将死去的华年。
——《在我的故乡我如觉得无聊》

他们已倦于城市辉煌 / 003

北征的纵队 / 007

天明在战壕里 / 009

伦敦 / 012

海外乡思 / 014

山上 / 016

鹰形的星群在天顶上翱翔 / 018

在船坞上 / 021

渡过沙洲 / 022

看异邦的人 / 024

冲击、冲击、冲击 / 026

鱼的天堂 / 028

空屋 / 032

爱情的花园 / 033

园里的树 / 035

东方的朝圣者 / 036

在我的故乡我如觉得无聊 / 040

辑二

你炽烈地发光，照得夜晚的森林灿烂辉煌。
——《老虎》

初春 / 045

泥块和小石子 / 047

最可爱的树 / 049

百合花 / 051

啊！向日葵 / 052

穷人的猪 / 053

秋 / 055

丛丛的荆棘 / 056

虻虫 / 057

病玫瑰 / 059

一颗毒树 / 060

我漂亮的玫瑰树 / 062

狐 / 063

老虎 / 064

雪 / 066

最后的雪 / 068

太阳落下去了 / 070

石凝 / 071

大地的回答 / 073

辑三

也许那个幻想有如实有,也许那个幻想像得不够。
——《梭罗门与巫女》

我的父母 / 077

保姆之歌 / 079

扫烟囱的孩子 / 080

流浪儿 / 082

小学生 / 084

一个小男孩的迷失 / 088

一个小女孩的迷失 / 090

小女孩的迷失 / 094

小女孩的寻获 / 099

空洞的人 / 104

苦行者 / 112

雪岭上的苦行人 / 114

古行吟诗人的声音 / 115

我已故的公爵夫人 / 117

列宁 / 121

梭罗门与巫女 / 123

辑四

> 我一下子跳进这危险的世界：无依无靠，光着身，尖声喊叫，就像躲在云彩里的一个魔妖。
>
> ——《婴儿的悲哀》

诞辰 / 129

婴儿的悲哀 / 131

五月 / 132

空袭 / 134

爱尔兰空军驾驶员 / 136

暴露 / 138

飞天夜叉（空袭后写成）/ 142

回营时听见天鹨的歌声 / 145

资本家最后的统治方法 / 147

孩子们的哭声 / 149

在西班牙被炸死的儿童 / 162

你脸上的水 / 164

我的愿望 / 166

将死者的歌 / 167

一个死在战争里的人 / 169

送葬 / 170

升天节 / 171

咏希朗十四行诗 / 173

希朗的囚徒 / 175

天使 / 203

记忆 / 205

人生 / 207

辑五

> 一点，一点，展开在人手上，人能观察宇宙的横切面，用再多一点忍耐和时间。
> ——《人几乎能够》

夜晚在我周围暗下来 / 211

栗树落下火炬似的繁英 / 213

我独自坐着 / 217

我的心充满了忧愁 / 219

我不断地想到 / 220

人的抽象观念 / 222

为人道主义辩护 / 223

象征 / 227

歌 / 228

序诗 / 229

歌 / 231

和声歌辞 / 233

人几乎能够 / 235

我是唯一的人 / 237

一个圣像 / 240

入睡 / 241

AGA / 243

墓铭 / 245

给得撒 / 247

后记 / 249

辑一

在我随意游荡的每条路上,与我一同走,
向同一的方向,有那幽美而将死去的华年。
——《在我的故乡我如觉得无聊》

他们已倦于城市辉煌

当他们已倦于城市辉煌,
和地位的争取,终于委顿,
悬挂着轻松的锁链,等到
死也尊荣清道夫的时候。
富人的街道,任意的喜爱,
皆如旧衣褪了色,死行过,
露着白齿,经过一切人脸,
清洁,平等,如雪上的光辉。

现在当愁郁在四围冻结,
当痛苦的光在街角闪耀,
那些人,此时金色的栋梁,
藏在衣服里,当然从饥饿
我们能击火,如火石一样。
我们的力量是筋骨的力,
清洁,平等,如雪上的光辉。
也是饥饿和不得已的力,
也是我们彼此相爱的力。

读这奇异的语言的人们,
我们终于来到一个国家,
这里平等照耀,如雪的光。
在这里,你们也许会诧异,
工场,金钱,利润,建筑,如何
能够藏起人间显然的爱?

同志们，不要让后来的人，
我们所生的美盛的后代，
怀疑，当银行、教会、统治欲，
都失败了以后，我们缺少
如茁出向着流泉的草木，
如猛虎的春天一般的力，
在古旧的机构的残余中，
让他们看这惊叹的晨光
在四围爆炸，令人目迷眩。

After They Have Tired of the Brilliance of Cities

After they have tired of the brilliance of cities
And of striving for office where at last they may languish
Hung round with easy chains until
Death and Jerusalem glorify also the crossing-sweeper:
Then those streets the rich built and their easy love
Fade like old cloths, and it is death stalks through life
Grinning white through all faces
Clean and equal like the shine from snow.

In this time when grief pours freezing over us,
When the hard light of pain gleams at every street corner,
When those who were pillars of that day's gold roof
Shrink in their clothes; surely from hunger
We may strike fire, like fire from flint?
And our strength is now the strength of our bones
Clean and equal like the shine from snow
And the strength of fame and our enforced idleness,
And it is the strength of our love for each other.

Readers of this strange language
We have come at last to a country
Where light equal, like the shine from snow, strikes all faces,
Here you may wonder
How it was that works, money, interest, building, could ever hide
The palpable and obvious love of man for man.

Oh comrades, let not those who follow after
—The beautiful generation that shall spring from our sides—
Let them not wonder how after the failure of banks

The failure of cathedrals and the declared insanity of our rulers,
We lacked the Spring-like resources of the tiger
Or of plants who strike out new roots to gushing waters.
But through torn-down portions of old fabric let their eyes
Watch the admiring dawn explode like a shell
Around us, dazing us with its light like the shine from snow.

斯蒂芬·史彭德 / 作
Stephen Spender, 1909—1995

杨宪益 / 译

北征的纵队

角声在岩石的谷里蜷曲着,
在鸷鸟的鸣声里得到回响。
迫害又加于苦痛的人群上,
人白白死去,没有光荣事迹。

十一天这纵队走过了荒田,
经过焚毁的农村,空院,断桥。
荒凉在面前有如阴影动摇,
劫灰如雨。他们的焦虑日添。

步入北方的黑暗里,渐走近
一条窄径,山水可怖的冲流,
阴影淤结的恐吓,和多端的
死路,都埋伏好了,等待他们。

最后的前卫吹出凄凉角声,
纵队已迷失了,后继再无人。

A Northern Legion

Bugle calls coiling through the rocky valley
have found echoes in the eagles' cries:
an outrage is done on anguish'd men
now men die and death is no deedful glory.

Eleven days this legion forced the ruin'd fields, the
burnt homesteads and empty garths, the broken arches
of bridges: desolation moving like a shadow before them, a
rain of ashes. Endless their anxiety.

Marching into a northern darkness: approaching
a narrow defile, the waters falling fearfully
the clotting menace of shadows and all the multiple
instruments of death in ambush against them.

The last of the vanguard sounds his doleful note.
The legion now is lost. None will follow.

赫伯特·里德 / 作
Herbert Read, 1893—1968
杨宪益 / 译

天明在战壕里

夜的黑暗渐渐消灭了,
这还是那古老的时间。
有活东西跳到我手上,
是一个滑稽的小老鼠,
当我摘战壕上罂粟花,
来插在我耳后的时候。
小东西,他们会枪毙你,
如他们知道你的同情,
天知道,你还反对什么。
你接触了英国人的手,
也许再触德国人的手,
无疑的,不久如你高兴,
你会走过中间的草地。
大概你自己心里好笑,
经过明眸,健硕的身体,
他们活的希望比你少,
为你杀戮的一念所牵制,
在大地的腹中卧藏着,
在被战争蹂躏的田野,
你在我眼里看见什么?
当钢片与火焰狂叫着,
由天空中掷来的时候。
怎样的战栗?怎样心悸?
在人脉搏里的红罂粟,
时时的落下,落下,落下。
只我耳边的还是无恙,
沾了一点灰,有一点白。

Break of Day in the Trenches

The darkness crumbles away.
It is the same old druid Time as ever,
Only a live thing leaps my hand,
A queer sardonic rat,
As I pull the parapet's poppy
To stick behind my ear.
Droll rat, they would shoot you if they knew
Your cosmopolitan sympathies.
Now you have touched this English hand
You will do the same to a German
Soon, no doubt, if it be your pleasure
To cross the sleeping green between.
It seems you inwardly grin as you pass
Strong eyes, fine limbs, haughty athletes,
Less chanced than you for life,
Bonds to the whims of murder,
Sprawled in the bowels of the earth,
The torn fields of France.
What do you see in our eyes
At the shrieking iron and flame
Hurled through still heavens?
What quaver—what heart aghast?
Poppies whose roots are in man's veins
Drop, and are ever dropping;
But mine in my ear is safe—
Just a little white with the dust.

艾萨克·罗森堡 / 作
Isaac Rosenberg, 1890—1918
杨宪益 / 译

ZH LONG DON
2012.4.

伦敦

我漫步走过每一条特辖的街道，
附近有那特辖的泰晤士河流过，
在我所遇到的每一张脸上，我看到
衰弱的痕迹与悲痛的痕迹交错。

每一个成人的每一声呼喊，
每一个幼儿恐惧的惊叫，
在每一个声音、每一道禁令里面，
我都听到心灵铸成的镣铐。

那扫烟囱的孩子怎样地哭喊，
震骇了每一座变黑了的教堂，
还有那倒运的兵士们的悲叹
带着鲜血顺着宫墙往下流淌。

但更多的是在午夜的街道上我听见，
那年轻的娼妓是怎样地诅咒，
摧残了新生婴儿的眼泪，
用疫疠把新婚的枢车摧毁。

London

I wandered through each chartered street,
Near where the chartered Thames does flow,
And mark in every face I meet,
Marks of weakness, marks of woe.

In every cry of every man,
In every infant's cry of fear,
In every voice, in every ban,
The mind-forged manacles I hear:

How the chimney-sweeper's cry
Every blackening church appals,
And the hapless soldier's sigh
Runs in blood down palace-walls.

But most, through midnight streets I hear
How the youthful harlot's curse
Blasts the new-born infant's tear,
And blights with plagues the marriage-hearse.

威廉・布莱克 / 作
William Blake, 1757—1827
杨苡 / 译

海外乡思

啊,要是在英格兰,
那儿现在正是四月。
早上不管是谁醒来在英格兰,
便可看见,不知不觉,
那最低的枝子和灌木丛,
环绕着榆树干,嫩叶初生,
那时燕雀在果园枝头歌唱,
在英格兰——就在这时光!

四月过后,跟着就是五月,
白喉雀筑巢,还有所有的燕子!
听吧,就在我那向田野倾斜着的篱笆边,
我的开着花的梨树在苜蓿草上撒遍
花朵和露珠。在那弯身的枝头一端,
那是聪明的画眉鸟,它要把每只歌唱两遍
不然你要以为它永不会重新获得,
那第一次的无忧无虑的疯狂的欢乐!
虽然田野因露水晶晶而显得崎岖不平,
一切将很愉快,当晌午重新唤醒
那些金凤花,宛如小孩子的财宝一样,
这俗艳的番木瓜花可远不如它漂亮。

Home-Thoughts, from Abroad

Oh, to be in England
Now that April's there,
And whoever wakes in England
Sees, some morning, unaware,
That the lowest boughs and the brushwood sheaf
Round the elm-tree bole are in tiny leaf,
While the chaffinch sings on the orchard bough
In England—now!

And after April, when May follows,
And the whitethroat builds, and all the swallows!
Hark, where my blossomed pear-tree in the hedge
Leans to the field and scatters on the clover
Blossoms and dewdrops—at the bent spray's edge—
That's the wise thrush; he sings each song twice over,
Lest you should think he never could recapture
The first fine careless rapture!
And though the fields look rough with hoary dew,
All will be gay when noontide wakes anew
The buttercups, the little children's dower
—Far brighter than this gaudy melon-flower!

罗伯特·勃朗宁 / 作
Robert Browning, 1812—1889
杨苡 / 译

山上

喘着气,我们倒在风吹的山上。
在阳光里笑,吻那可爱的绿草。
你说,"荣耀,欢乐,我们都经过了,
还有春风,太阳,大地,还有鸟唱,
我们老了的时候","当我们死去,
我们的一切消灭,生命还燃着,
在别人心中,别人唇上"。我就说:
"爱,我们的天堂,就在此时,此处。
我们是大地最好的,在此受训,
生命是我们呼声,遵守着任务,
我们将走下坡,以坚决的足步
戴着华冠,走入黑暗。"我们自信,
笑着,因我们有如此的话可说,
可是你忽然哭了,又把头扭过。

The Hill

Breathless, we flung us on the windy hill,
Laughed in the sun, and kissed the lovely grass.
You said "Through glory and ecstasy we pass;
Wind, sun, and earth remain, and birds sing still,
When we are old, are old...." "And when we die
All's over that is ours; and life burns on
Through other lovers, other lips" said I,
"Heart of my heart, our heaven is now, is won!"
"We are Earth's best, that learnt her lesson here.
Life is our cry. We have kept the faith!" we said;
"We shall go down with unreluctant tread
Rose-crowned into the darkness!".... Proud we were,
And laughed, that had such brave true things to say.
And then you suddenly cried, and turned away.

鲁珀特·布鲁克 / 作
Rupert Brooke, 1887—1915
杨苡 / 译

鹰形的星群在天顶上翱翔

鹰形的星群在天顶上翱翔,
猎人同他的狗循着轨道追,
啊,图像的星群,永久的转动,
啊,定命的时季,永久的来复,
啊,春天,秋天,生于死的世界,
观念与行动,无穷尽的循环,
无尽的发明,和无尽的试验,
给人动作,不给无动的知识,
给人语言,不给无言的知识,
给人道理而不使人明白道,
所有的知识使人更不了解,
不了解,使得人们更近死亡,
离死亡近,并不是离上帝近。
生活中失去的生命在哪里?
知识中失去的智慧在哪里?
见闻中失去的知识在哪里?
在二十世纪里天体的循环
使人更远离上帝,更近尘土。

The Eagle Soars in the Summit of Heaven

The Eagle soars in the summit of Heaven,
The Hunter with his dogs pursues his circuit.
O perpetual revolution of configured stars,
O perpetual recurrence of determined seasons,
O world of spring and autumn, birth and dying!
The endless cycle of idea and action,
Endless invention, endless experiment,
Brings knowledge of motion, but not of stillness;
Knowledge of speech, but not of silence;
Knowledge of words, and ignorance of the Word.
All our knowledge brings us nearer to our ignorance,
All our ignorance brings us nearer to death,
But nearness to death no nearer to GOD
Where is the Life we have lost in living?
Where is the wisdom we have lost in knowledge?
Where is the knowledge we have lost in information?
The cycles of Heaven in twenty centuries
Bring us farther from GOD and nearer to the Dust.

I journeyed to London, to the timekept City,
Where the River flows, with foreign notations.
There I was told: we have too many churches,
And too few chop-houses. There I was told:
Let the vicars retire. Men do not need the Church
In the place where they work, but where they spend their Sundays.
In the City, we need no bells:
Let them waken the suburbs.
I journeyed to the suburbs, and there I was told:
We toil for six days, on the seventh we must motor

To Hindhead, or Maidenhead.
If the weather is foul we stay at home and read the paper.
In industrial districts, there I was told
Of economic laws.
In the pleasant countryside, there it seemed
That the country now is only fit for picnics.
And the Church does not seem to be wanted
In country or in suburb; and in the town
Only for important weddings.

T. S. 艾略特 / 作
T. S. Eliot, 1888—1965

杨宪益 / 译

在船坞上

午夜时,在寂静的船坞上,
缠绕在高桅系绳的尖端,
悬挂着月亮。看起来很远,
小儿的气球,嬉戏后遗忘。

Above the Dock

Above the quiet dock in mid night,
Tangled in the tall mast's corded height,
Hangs the moon. What seemed so far away
Is but a child's balloon, forgotten after play.

T. E. 休姆 / 作
T. E. Hulme, 1883—1917

杨宪益 / 译

渡过沙洲

夕阳和晚星,
有声音呼唤我!
但愿沙洲没有呜咽声
当我出海漂泊。

却有潮汐缓行仿佛入睡,
岂容波涛汹涌,
当从无垠深处挣脱又转回
重新回归洲中。

黄昏与晚钟声,
而后便是黑暗!
但愿没有诀别的悲痛,
当我启航扬帆。

脱离我们的时空界限,
潮水带我远游,
我盼望和我的舵手见面,
当我渡过沙洲。

Crossing the Bar

Sunset and evening star,
And one clear call for me!
And may there be no moaning of the bar,
When I put out to sea,

But such a tide as moving seems asleep,
Too full for sound and foam,
When that which drew from out the boundless deep
Turns again home.

Twilight and evening bell,
And after that the dark!
And may there be no sadness of farewell,
When I embark;

For tho' from out our bourne of Time and Place
The flood may bear me far,
I hope to see my Pilot face to face
When I have crost the bar.

阿弗莱·丁尼生 / 作
Alfred Tennyson, 1809—1892
杨宪益 / 译

看异邦的人

看,异邦的人,现在看这个岛,
发现那供你欣赏的动跃的波光。
静立在这里,
也不要发声,
为了在你的耳中
可以如同溪水一般流荡着,
大海的摇曳的声音。

且略流连于这田畦的终尾,
有白垩的石岩落入浪花,与它的
突起的平岩。
对着潮汐的
牵拽,和它的撞击,
卵石在吸引的海水后匍匐着,
海鸥在峭崖上小息。

远远看来,有如漂着的种子,
船只分去,向着急促自动的目的。
这一切景象
能冲流动荡,
在记忆中,如现在
这些云流过海港的一面明镜,
终夏在海水里徘徊。

Look, Stranger

Look, stranger, at this island now
The leaping light for your delight discovers,
Stand stable here
And silent be,
That through the channels of the ear
May wander like a river
The swaying sound of the sea.

Here are the small field's ending pause
Where the chalk wall falls to the foam, and its tall ledges
Oppose the pluck
And knock of the tide,
And the shingle scrambles after the suck-
ing surf,
And the gull lodges
A moment on its sheer side.

Far off like floating seeds the ships
Diverge on urgent voluntary errands;
And the full view
Indeed may enter
And move in memory as now these clouds do,
That pass the harbour mirror
And all the summer through the water saunter.

W. H. 奥登 / 作
W. H. Auden, 1907—1973
杨宪益 / 译

冲击、冲击、冲击

冲击、冲击、冲击,
在你冰冷的灰灰的石头上,啊,海洋!
但愿我能用言语表达出
我的心里涌现的种种思想。

啊,那渔夫孩子多么好呀,
他可以和他妹妹游玩时大叫大嚷!
啊,那当水手的小伙子多么好呀,
他在海湾中他的小船里放声歌唱!

那些宏伟的船只驶向
山脚下它们的避风港。
啊,但愿能触摸一只已消失的手,
但愿能听到已静寂的声响!

冲击、冲击、冲击,
在你的岩石脚下,啊,海洋!
但那一天已逝去,它那温柔的魅力,
再也不会回到我的身旁!

Break, Break, Break

Break, break, break,
On thy cold gray stones, O Sea!
And I would that my tongue could utter
The thoughts that arise in me.

O, well for the fisherman's boy,
That he shouts with his sister at play!
O, well for the sailor lad,
That he sings in his boat on the bay!

And the stately ships go on
To their haven under the hill;
But O for the touch of a vanished hand,
And the sound of a voice that is still!

Break, break, break,
At the foot of thy crags, O Sea!
But the tender grace of a day that is dead
Will never come back to me.

阿弗莱·丁尼生 / 作
Alfred Tennyson, 1809—1892
杨宪益 / 译

鱼的天堂

鱼吃饱了苍蝇,在六月天,
中午时分,在水里面流连,
研究深奥智慧,或暗或明,
一切所要,或所怕的事情。
鱼就说:"我们有了河同溪,
这外面难道能没有东西?
生命不是一切,我们坚持。
因为那样岂不太无意思?
所以不能怀疑,总有至善,
从那泥和水的里面出现。
心诚的人一定也能看到,
在流动着的水里有至道,
所以根据信仰,我们呼唤,
未来的世界总不会太干。
泥土归于泥土,死亡来近,
生命的终了不在此决定,
而是在宇宙之外某一地,
有更湿的水,更烂的烂泥。
那里我们相信,有神游戏,
江河未生时,它就在那里,
伟大而有鱼的形状,心情。
全能而仁善,身上也有鳞,
而在那伟大的鱼鳍下面,
最小的小鱼也可以流连。
那里的苍蝇永不藏鱼钩。"

鱼说:"那就是永久的河流,
那里有比这里多的水草,
那里的泥也非常的美好,
有肥的蠋虫在四围漂流,
极好的蛴螬也在水里头,
有不死的蛾,不死的苍蝇,
又有蛆虫也是永远长生,
那是我们所希望的至乐,
也不再有土地。"鱼如此说。

Heaven

Fish (fly-replete, in depth of June,
Dawdling away their wat'ry noon)
Ponder deep wisdom, dark or clear,
Each secret fishy hope or fear.
Fish say, they have their Stream and Pond;
But is there anything Beyond?
This life cannot be All, they swear,
For how unpleasant, if it were!
One may not doubt that, somehow, Good
Shall come of Water and of Mud;
And, sure, the reverent eye must see
A Purpose in Liquidity.
We darkly know, by Faith we cry,
The future is not Wholly Dry.
Mud unto mud!-Death eddies nearm dash
Not here the appointed End, not here!
But somewhere, beyond Space and Time,
Is wetter water, slimier slime!
And there (they trust) there swimmeth One
Who swam ere rivers were begun,
Immense, of fishy form and mind,
Squamous, omnipotent, and kind;
And under that Almighty Fin,
The littlest fish may enter in.
Oh! never fly conceals a hook,
Fish say, in the Eternal Brook,
But more than mundane weeds are there,
And mud, celestially fair;
Fat caterpillars drift around,

And Paradisal grubs are found;
Unfading moths, immortal flies,
And the worm that never dies.
And in that heaven of all their wish,
There shall be no more land, say fish.

鲁珀特·布鲁克 / 作
Rupert Brooke, 1887—1915
杨苡 / 译

空屋

时钟解释着标点和章句,
钟的声音干窄,重复述说,
钟辩论着,一位教授讲学,
高声,竖起一指,已下课了。

时间,光景,从这屋里流过,
如人摘着花,如人嘴吹着,
不成音调,如在火前闲谈,
如妇人织衣,如小儿裁纸。

Empty Room

The clock disserts on punctuation, syntax.
The clock's voice, thin and dry, asserts, repeats.
The clock insists: a lecturer demonstrating,
Loudly, with finger raised, when the class has gone.
But time flows through the room, light flows through the room
Like someone picking flowers, like someone whistling
Without a tune, like talk in front of a fire,
Like a woman knitting or a child snipping at paper.

A. S. J. 太息蒙 / 作
A. S. J. Tessimond, 1902—1962

杨宪益 / 译

爱情的花园

我去到爱情的花园里,
看见了我从未见过的情景:
在我经常玩耍的草地,
有一座礼拜堂建立在中心。

这礼拜堂的大门紧紧关闭,
门上写着,你不准如何如何,
于是我转身到爱情的花园里,
那里盛开着许多可爱的花朵,

我却看见那儿尽是坟墓,
墓碑代替了原有的花朵:
穿黑袍的牧师还在踱来踱去,
用荆棘捆住了我的欲念和欢乐。

The Garden of Love

I went to the Garden of Love,
And saw what I never had seen;
A Chapel was built in the midst,
Where I used to play on the green.

And the gates of this Chapel were shut
And "Thou shalt not," writ over the door;
So I turned to the Garden of Love
That so many sweet flowers bore.

And I saw it was filled with graves,
And tombstones where flowers should be;
And priests in black gowns were walking their rounds,
And binding with briars my joys and desires.

威廉·布莱克 / 作
William Blake, 1757—1827
杨苡 / 译

园里的树

那里有一株生在西域的树,
或在东方,离天堂的树不远。
它的僵冷的外壳,不按节气,
不肯轻易地脱离它的母亲,
只在火燃的树林里才成熟。
如往日酒神那样出世,等待
在人生中时间终了的表象。
我知火生的金翅鸟是植物。
酒神的母亲,曾经求神降临,
如这树渴望着红色的晨光。

(英文版本未找到)

威廉·恩普森 / 作
William Empson, 1906—1984
杨宪益 / 译

东方的朝圣者

"我们去的时候天气很冷,
正是一年里最坏的时候,
去朝圣,而且路程这样远,
道路也崎岖,天气也严酷,
因为那正是三冬的时候。"
骆驼也疲乏了,蹄茧,局缩,
都卧倒在融化的冰雪里。
有的时候,我们也曾后悔,
离弃了山上的行宫庭圃,
和锦衣擎着酒浆的少女。
驼夫们也咒骂埋怨我们,
逃走,要他们的酒和女人。
夜间火炬熄灭,荫盖不足,
每城每镇都敌视着我们,
村庄也都龌龊,要高价钱,
我们那时真是非常困苦,
后来觉得不如夜里走路,
有时候偷点空闲来睡觉,
有声音在我们耳里鸣着,
说这些都是傻子的事情。

黎明,我们来到一个山谷,
潮湿,无雪,有草木的芳馨;
有流泉,水磨撞击着黑暗,

在天低处,远远有三株树,
一匹老白马在草上奔驰,
一家酒店门楣挂着葡萄叶,
六只手门前掷骰子赌钱,
又有人脚踢着空的酒囊。
找不到消息,我们继续走,
黄昏才找到,一点也不早,
正好找着,可以说是满意,
这都是很久的事,我记得,
我也愿再来一次,先写下
这事,先写下
这事,我们去那么远,为了
生?还是为了死?不错,是生,
我有证据,我看过生和死。
我曾以为是不同,这次生
是我们的苦痛,好像是死。
我们回到我们的王国去,
度着旧生活,再不觉安宁,
看着异族人民抱着偶像,
我真希望再有一次的死。

The Journey of the Magi

'A cold coming we had of it,
Just the worst time of the year
For a journey, and such a long journey:
The ways deep and the weather sharp,
The very dead of winter.'
And the camels galled, sorefooted, refractory,
Lying down in the melting snow.
There were times we regretted
The summer palaces on slopes, the terraces,
And the silken girls bringing sherbet.
Then the camel men cursing and grumbling
And running away, and wanting their liquor and women,
And the night-fires going out, and the lack of shelters,
And the cities hostile and the towns unfriendly
And the villages dirty and charging high prices:
A hard time we had of it.
At the end we preferred to travel all night,
Sleeping in snatches,
With the voices singing in our ears, saying
That this was all folly.

Then at dawn we came down to a temperate valley,
Wet, below the snow line, smelling of vegetation;
With a running stream and a water-mill beating the darkness,
And three trees on the low sky,
And an old white horse galloped away in the meadow.
Then we came to a tavern with vine-leaves over the lintel,
Six hands at an open door dicing for pieces of silver,
And feet kicking the empty wine-skins.

But there was no information, and so we continued
And arriving at evening, not a moment too soon
Finding the place; it was (you might say) satisfactory.

All this was a long time ago, I remember,
And I would do it again, but set down
This set down
This: were we led all that way for
Birth or Death? There was a Birth, certainly
We had evidence and no doubt. I had seen birth and death,
But had thought they were different; this Birth was
Hard and bitter agony for us, like Death, our death.
We returned to our places, these Kingdoms,
But no longer at ease here, in the old dispensation,
With an alien people clutching their gods.
I should be glad of another death.

T. S. 艾略特 / 作
T. S. Eliot, 1888—1965
杨宪益 / 译

在我的故乡我如觉得无聊

在我的故乡，我如觉得无聊，
我还有方法安慰我的寂寥，
因为我心苦痛的缘故，大地
也为她所生的儿孙而哀泣。
还有矗立的山丘，千古常存，
分我痛苦，安慰有涯的人生。
在我随意游荡的每条路上，
与我一同走，向同一的方向，
有那幽美而将死去的华年，
很亲密的随从，在我的身边。
有时我在幽暗的山林经过，
我听见山榉实萧萧的下堕，
我又看见绛紫的番红花朵，
在秋天的幽谷里面怒放着。
或看见散在春暮的田野间，
白色的女裙花寂寂的安眠，
有如一湾反映天空的春水，
林里的蓝钟花笼着薄霭睡。
在乡间的路上，除这些以外，
有不同季节，来消我的块垒。
可是在城里街上，我无处寻
如此的伴侣，除了那些闲人。
即使他们情愿，他们也不
急急来接受旁人的忧愁，
他们已有足够的了。我看见

在许多揣度我的眼睛里面，
因太缺少欢乐，而失了同情，
那一种心理的不治的重病。
为苦痛所逼迫，他们只能够
去怨恨他们的一切的朋友；
在他们自己死前，他们只能
望着你，而希冀你交着恶运。

In My Own Shire, If I Was Sad

In my own shire, if I was sad,
Homely comforters I had:
The earth, because my heart was sore,
Sorrowed for the son she bore;
And standing hills, long to remain,
Shared their short-lived comrade's pain.
And bound for the same bourn as I,
On every road I wandered by,
Trod beside me, close and dear,
The beautiful and death-struck year:
Whether in the woodland brown
I heard the beechnut rustle down,
And saw the purple crocus pale
Flower about the autumn dale;
Or littering far the fields of May
Lady-smocks a-bleaching lay,
And like a skylit water stood
The bluebells in the azured wood.
Yonder, lightening other loads,
The seasons range the country roads,
But here in London streets I ken
No such helpmates, only men;
And these are not in plight to bear,
If they would, another's care.
They have enough as 'tis: I see
In many an eye that measures me
The mortal sickness of a mind
Too unhappy to be kind.
Undone with misery, all they can
Is to hate their fellow man;
And till they drop they needs must still
Look at you and wish you ill.

A. E. 豪斯曼 / 作
A. E. Housman, 1859—1936

杨宪益 / 译

辑二

你炽烈地发光,照得夜晚的森林灿烂辉煌
——《老虎》

初春

飞击啊,雪,那黑鸟的喋喋,
你无法阻止它将唱的歌。
不眠的东风,你不能吹灭
榲桲花,杏花,
小的紫风信子的
团团的花蕊,
李花的新叶,你无可如何。
百合的花茎不中止生长,
有精液在风吹的花丛里,
雪掩的矮林里,冻得发狂。
一个鸫鸟歌唱着,说"可惜"。

爱,余下的春天没有许多。
在春去的时候,数着它们,
使我们更明白余下几何。
不但东风和雪,我希望能
挽回来那些失去的时间,
那些带来蜂和花的日子。
我宁愿使严霜寒夜留连,
只要我们能把春天遏止。

Eager Spring

Whirl, snow, on the blackbird's chatter;
You will not hinder his song to come.
East wind, Sleepless, you cannot scatter
Quince-bud, almond-bud,
Little grape-hyacinth's
Clustering brood,
Nor unfurl the tips of the plum.
No half-born stalk of lily stops;
There is sap in the storm-torn bush;
And, ruffled by gusts in a snowblurred copse,
" Pity to wait" sings a thrush.

Love, there are few Springs left for us;
They go, and the count of them as they go
Makes surer the count that is left for us.
More than the East wind, more than the snow,
I would put back these hours that bring
Buds and bees and are lost;
I would hold the night and the frost,
To save for us one more Spring.

戈登·博顿利 / 作
Gordon Bottomley, 1874—1948
杨宪益 / 译

泥块和小石子

"爱情并不想讨它自己欢欣,
对它自己也丝毫不挂心,
只是为了别人才舍弃安宁,
在地狱的绝望中建立一座天庭。"

一小块泥巴就这样唱着,
它被牛羊群的脚踩来踩去,
但是溪流里有一块小石子,
它用颤音唱出了合拍的诗句。

"爱情只想讨它自己的欢欣,
随心所欲地去束缚别人:
它看到别人失去安宁就高兴,
建立一座地狱来对抗天庭。"

The Clod and the Pebble

"Love seeketh not itself to please,
Nor for itself hath any care,
But for another gives its ease,
And builds a heaven in hell's despair."

So sung a little clod of clay,
Trodden with the cattle's feet;
But a pebble of the brook
Warbled out these meters meet:

"Love seeketh only Self to please,
To bind another to its delight,
Joys in another's loss of ease,
And builds a hell in heaven's despite."

威廉·布莱克 / 作
William Blake, 1757—1827
杨苡 / 译

最可爱的树

最可爱的树,樱桃,如今
枝上已经垂下了繁英,
孤立在这幽林野径里,
为这佳节穿上了白衣。

在我的七十流年里面,
有二十年总不会再见,
从七十春天里去二十,
我只余下五十个春日。

五十春天既然是很少,
去赏玩开花的树或草,
我要到林径间去玩耍,
去看樱桃树如雪的花。

Loveliest of Trees

Loveliest of trees, the cherry now
Is hung with bloom along the bough,
And stands about the woodland ride
Wearing white for Eastertide.

Now of my threescore years and ten,
Twenty will not come again,
And take from seventy springs a score,
It only leaves me fifty more.

And since to look at things in bloom
Fifty springs are little room,
About the woodlands I will go
To see the cherry hung with snow.

A. E. 豪斯曼 / 作
A. E. Housman, 1859—1936
杨宪益 / 译

百合花

含羞的玫瑰生出一根刺，
驯顺的羔羊有双吓人的角。
白色的百合花却陶醉在爱情里，
没有刺或恐吓污她的美好。

The Lily

The modest Rose puts forth a thorn,
The humble sheep a threat'ning horn:
While the Lily white shall in love delight,
Nor a thorn nor a threat stain her beauty bright.

威廉·布莱克 / 作
William Blake, 1757—1827
杨苡 / 译

啊！向日葵

啊，向日葵！你厌倦了时光。
它计数着太阳的脚步：
你寻找那美好的宝贵的地方，
在那里旅人结束了他的征途。

在那里因情欲而憔悴的青年，
和那苍白的裹着雪白尸衣的姑娘：
从他们的坟墓中升起，渴望
我的向日葵所向往的地方。

Ah! Sunflower

Ah Sunflower, weary of time,
Who countest the steps of the sun;
Seeking after that sweet golden clime
Where the traveller's journey is done;

Where the Youth pined away with desire,
And the pale virgin shrouded in snow,
Arise from their graves, and aspire
Where my Sunflower wishes to go!

威廉·布莱克 / 作
William Blake, 1757—1827
杨苡 / 译

穷人的猪

已经有黄梅的落英点缀田园,
苹果树干斑斓如老蟾蜍的背,
着了小的红花,在玫瑰未开前。
筑着新巢的鹈鸟,看着老人堆
在有阳光的篱上青皮的柳条。
关起的母猪听见他走过,就叫,
要把门闩推开,从里面向外逃,
但它有环的嘴,使它不能乱跑。

后来他放它出来跑,鼻子直喷;
鼓起力量,它就跑到茅舍门口,
做出饥饿的呼声,求冷肴残羹;
它有如一阵旋风,又乱撞乱走,
用鼻撩拨着狗,使得鸡雏奔飞;
玩腻时,又如小孩一样撅着嘴。

The Poor Man's Pig

Already fallen plum-bloom stars the green
And apple-boughs as knarred as old toads' backs
Wear their small roses ere a rose is seen;
The building thrush watches old Job who stacks
The bright-peeled osiers on the sunny fence,
The pent sow grunts to hear him stumping by,
And tries to push the bolt and scamper thence,
But her ringed snout still keeps her to the sty.

Then out he lets her run; away she snorts
In bundling gallop for the cottage door,
With hungry hubbub begging crusts and orts,
Then like the whirlwind bumping round once more;
Nuzzling the dog, making the pullets run,
And sulky as a child when her play's done.

埃德蒙·布伦顿 / 作
Edmund Blundun, 1896—1974

杨宪益 / 译

秋

秋夜里一点寒意。
我到外面散步,
看见赤色的月倚在篱边,
如一红脸的村夫。
我没停止说话,只点点头,
四围有憧憬的星,
脸白,如城里小儿。

Autumn

A touch of cold in the Autumn night—
I walked abroad,
And saw the ruddy moon lean over a hedge
Like a red-faced farmer.
I did not stop to speak, but nodded,
And round about were the wistful stars
With white faces like town children.

T. E. 休姆 / 作
T. E. Hulme, 1883—1917

杨宪益 / 译

丛丛的荆棘

丛丛的荆棘藏起,每年春天
都是如此,锈了的铁耙,一杆
早就用坏的锄头,一个石碾。
只有榆树还突出荆棘上面。

我也最喜欢农村的这一角,
正如同任何花一样的迷人。
我喜欢荆棘上常有的轻尘,
常有,除非要证明雨的美妙。

Tall Nettles

Tall nettles cover up, as they have done
These many springs, the rusty harrow, the plough
Long worn out, and the roller made of stone:
Only the elm butt tops the nettles now.

This corner of the farmyard I like most:
As well as any bloom upon a flower
I like the dust on the nettles, never lost
Except to prove the sweetness of a shower.

爱德华·托马斯 / 作
Edward Thomas, 1878—1917

杨宪益 / 译

虻虫

小小的虻虫,
你在夏天的游戏,
已被我的手,
不经意拂去。

我难道不是,
一个像你一样的虻虫?
你难道不是,
一个像我一样的人?

因为我跳舞,
喝酒又歌唱,
直到有只莽撞的手
掸掉了我的翅膀。

如若思想是生命,
是呼吸也是力量,
思想的贫乏,
便是死亡;

那么我就是个,
快活的虻虫,
无论我是死去,
或是我生存。

The Fly

Little fly,
Thy summer's play
My thoughtless hand
Has brushed away.

Am not I
A fly like thee?
Or art not thou
A man like me?

For I dance
And drink and sing,
Till some blind hand
Shall brush my wing.

If thought is life
And strength and breath,
And the want
Of thought is death,

Then am I
A happy fly,
If I live,
Or if I die.

威廉·布莱克 / 作
William Blake, 1757—1827
杨苡 / 译

病玫瑰

哦,玫瑰,你病了。
那看不见的小虫
飞翔在黑夜里,
在咆哮的暴风雨中:

发现了你的床
沉于猩红色的欢欣。
其黑色的秘密的爱情,
毁掉了你的生命。

The Sick Rose

O Rose, thou art sick!
The invisible worm
That flies in the night,
In the howling storm,

Has found out thy bed
Of crimson joy:
And his dark secret love
Does thy life destroy.

威廉·布莱克 / 作
William Blake, 1757—1827

杨苡 / 译

一颗毒树

我对我的朋友生气,
我说出来,愤怒就平息。
我对我的仇人气恼!
我并没说,愤怒却不断增长了。

我怀着恐惧给它浇水,
早早晚晚洒下我的眼泪:
我用微笑当太阳使它温暖,
捎带上我温柔而虚假的欺骗。

于是它白天黑夜长得不错,
直到它结成了一只漂亮的苹果。
我的仇人看见它鲜艳光泽,
他也知道那属于我。

便悄悄进了我的花园里,
当夜幕将天空遮蔽。
第二天清早我高兴地看到,
我的仇人直挺挺地躺在树下了。

A Poison Tree

I was angry with my friend:
I told my wrath, my wrath did end.
I was angry with my foe:
I told it not, my wrath did grow.

And I watered it in fears,
Night and morning with my tears;
And I sunned it with smiles,
And with soft deceitful wiles.

And it grew both day and night,
Till it bore an apple bright.
And my foe beheld it shine.
And he knew that it was mine,

And into my garden stole
When the night had veiled the pole;
In the morning glad I see
My foe outstretched beneath the tree.

威廉·布莱克 / 作
William Blake, 1757—1827
杨苡 / 译

我漂亮的玫瑰树

有人送给我一朵花,
五月里从没有这样的花,
但我说我有一棵漂亮的玫瑰树,
我就把这朵可爱的花送还给他。

然后我去看我漂亮的玫瑰树,
白天黑夜把她好好照应,
但我的玫瑰却嫉妒得掉头不顾,
而她的刺却成了我唯一的欢欣。

My Pretty Rose Tree

A flower was offered to me,
Such a flower as May never bore;
But I said "I've a pretty rose tree,"
And I passed the sweet flower o'er.

Then I went to my pretty rose tree,
To tend her by day and by night;
But my rose turned away with jealousy,
And her thorns were my only delight.

威廉·布莱克/作
William Blake, 1757—1827

杨苡/译

狐

利用夜间阴影,
他在篱间移匿。
一条动作蜷曲,
在它的梦想里。
呼声震动田野,
榛莽不足掩蔽。
猎人得到喜乐,
猎犬肩上一齿。
因绝望而紧张,
知道死期将至。
狂怒转成颓丧,
又把感觉抛弃。

(英文版本未找到)

克利福德·戴门特 / 作
Clifford Dyment, 1914—1971
杨宪益 / 译

老虎

老虎,老虎,你炽烈地发光,
照得夜晚的森林灿烂辉煌。
是什么样不朽的手或眼睛
造就你一身惊人的匀称?

在什么样遥远的海底或天边,
燃烧起你眼睛中的火焰?
凭借什么样的翅膀敢于凌空?
什么样的手竟然敢携取这个火种?

什么样的技巧,什么样的肩肘,
竟能拧成你心胸的肌肉?
而当你的心开始蹦跳,
什么样惊人的手、惊人的脚?

什么样的铁锤?什么样的铁链?
什么样的熔炉将你的头脑熔炼?
什么样的铁砧?什么样惊人的握力,
竟敢死死地抓住这些可怕的东西?

当星星射下它们的万道光辉,
又在天空上洒遍了点点珠泪,
看见他的杰作他可曾微笑?
不就是他造了你,一如他曾造过羊羔?

老虎,老虎,你炽烈地发光,
照得夜晚的森林灿烂辉煌:
是什么样的不朽的手或眼睛
能把你一身惊人的匀称造就?

The Tyger

Tyger! Tyger! burning bright
In the forest of the night;
What immortal hand or eye
Could frame thy fearful symmetry?

In what distant deeps or skies
Burnt the fire of thine eyes?
On what wings dare he aspire?
What the hand dare seize the fire?

And what shoulder, and what art,
Could twist the sinews of thy heart?
And when thy heart began to beat,
What dread hand? and what dread feet?

What the hammer? what the chain?
In what furnace was thy brain?
What the anvil? what dread grasp
Dare its deadly terrors clasp?

When the stars threw down their spears,
And watered heaven with their tears,
Did he smile his work to see?
Did he who made the lamb make thee?

Tyger! Tyger! burning bright
In the forests of the night,
What immortal hand or eye
Dare frame thy fearful symmetry?

威廉·布莱克 / 作
William Blake, 1757—1827
杨苡 / 译

雪

房子忽变华绚,大的突出的窗
生出雪的细卵,上贴着红玫瑰,
没有声音,是并行着,而又矛盾。
世界比我们想象的还要突然。

比我们想象的还要荒谬杂乱。
无可矫正的繁复。我剥开分析
一个橘子,吐出橘核,而感觉到
一切事物无常的迷醉的感觉。

火吐着焰,带着轻响,因为世界
是比人所想象的还要侮慢放佚。
在舌上,在眼上,在耳中,在手中,
雪与玫瑰之间的,不只是玻璃。

Snow

The room was suddenly rich and the great bay-window was
Spawning snow and pink roses against it
Soundlessly collateral and incompatible:
World is suddener than we fancy it.

World is crazier and more of it than we think,
Incorrigibly plural. I peel and portion
A tangerine and spit the pips and feel
The drunkenness of things being various.

And the fire flames with a bubbling sound for world
Is more spiteful and gay than one supposes—
On the tongue on the eyes on the ears in the palms of one's hands—
There is more than glass between the snow and the huge roses.

路易斯·麦克尼斯 / 作
Louis MacNiece, 1907—1963
杨宪益 / 译

最后的雪

残雪还流连着
堆在鸟萝的钝蹼上,
把树身一面涂白。
在这有阳光的路上,
新的无名东西出现,
有叶,有苞,下面有茎,
还有土块连在上面,
来指示它们的来因。
无花说出它的名字,
可是一条绿色的箭,
从地下穿过枯叶时,
一下就刺杀了冬天。

Last Snow

Although the snow still lingers
Heaped on the ivy's blunt webbed fingers
And painting tree-trunks on one side,
Here in this sunlit ride
The fresh unchristened things appear,
Leaf, spathe and stem,
With crumbs of earth clinging to them
To show the way they came
But no flower yet to tell their name,
And one green spear
Stabbing a dead leaf from below
Kills winter at a blow.

安德鲁·杨 / 作
Andrew Young, 1885—1971
杨宪益 / 译

太阳落下去了

太阳落下去了,如今那长长的草,
在晚风中凄凉地摇摆,
野鸟从那古老的灰石边飞开,
到温暖的角落里寻觅一个安身所在。

在这四周所有的寂寞景色之中
我什么也看不见,也听不见,
除了远方来的风
叹息着吹过这一片荒原。

The Sun Has Set

The sun has set, and the long grass now
Waves dreamily in the evening wind;
And the wild bird has flown from that old gray stone
In some warm nook a couch to find.

In all the lonely landscape round
I see no light and hear no sound,
Except the wind that far away
Come sighing o'er the healthy sea.

艾米莉·勃朗特 / 作
Emily Bronte, 1818—1848
杨苡 / 译

石凝

足踝上有借来的羽翼,
手中提着石凝的僵死,
这猛士就走进了大堂,
堂上的人都抬起头望,
他们的呼吸一时凝止,
堂上再没有蹿动践踏的声响。

正是如此,当朋友来时,
留下一本借的书或花,
而离开,生死都不相关,
你也好像是死去一般,
你也不敢去翻那本书的铅页,
或触那些花,那些暗中凝止的年华。

闭上你的眼睛,
你眼睫下有许多太阳,
或看那屋中的镜子里,
你可以看见无数眼睛,
人们古代的笑,用剪刀裁下,
藏在镜子里的。

晴天,阴天,他总来会我,
豪放的猛士提着魔头,
我在那里只听见那中止死灭的太阳,
不住的啾啾。

或者那昏黄的天色,是患疯症人的短褐,
令人觉得大地环绕那变暗的衣袜,如
一颠狂的灯蛾。

(英文版本未找到)

路易斯·麦克尼斯 / 作
Louis MacNeice, 1907—1963

杨宪益 / 译

大地的回答

大地抬起她的头,
从那可怕又阴郁的黑暗中抬起,
她的光辉已遁去:
僵硬的恐惧!
她的鬈发被灰灰的绝望遮蔽。

监禁在湿漉漉的海岸,
繁星的嫉妒将我的小窝保存。
冷酷又灰白,
哭泣着走来,
我听见古老人类的父亲。

人类的自私的父亲,
残酷的嫉妒的自私的胆战心惊,
能够使得
在夜里锁着的
青春的处女与晨星欢欣。

春天可掩饰它的欢乐,
当花苞和花朵都在成长?
播种者呢?
可在夜间播种?
或者庄稼汉也在夜间耕种?

打开这沉重的锁链,
它把我的周身骨头全冻僵
自私!虚荣!
永久的灭亡!
将捆绑着的爱情解放。

Earth's Answer

Earth raised up her head
From the darkness dread and drear,
Her light fled,
Stony, dread,
And her locks covered with grey despair.

"Prisoned on watery shore,
Starry jealousy does keep my den
Cold and hoar;
Weeping o're,
I hear the father of the ancient men.

"Selfish father of men!
Cruel, jealous, selfish fear!
Can delight,
Chained in night,
The virgins of youth and morning bear?

"Does spring hide its joy,
When buds and blossoms grow?
Does the sower
Sow by night,
Or the plowman in darkness plough?

"Break this heavy chain,
That does freeze my bones around!
Selfish, vain,
Eternal bane,
That free love with bondage bound."

威廉·布莱克 / 作
William Blake, 1757—1827
杨苡 / 译

辑三

也许那个幻想有如实有,也许那个幻想像得不够。

——《梭罗门与巫女》

我的父母

我的父母不许我同野孩子玩,
他们说粗话如石块,穿破衣服,
破得露出了腿。他们在街上跑,
他们爬山,在乡下的河里洗澡。

我怕他们甚于老虎,我怕他们
如铁的筋肉,摇动的手和膝盖,
紧紧压在我臂上。我怕他们指我,
粗鲁的在路上,摹仿着我口吃。

他们很灵巧,他们从篱后跳出。
如一群狗向我们的世界怒吠,
他们投泥块,我不看,假装微笑,
我愿意能宽宥他们,但他们不笑。

My Parents

My parents kept me from children who were rough
Who threw words like stones and wore torn clothes
Their thighs showed through rags they ran in the street
And climbed cliffs and stripped by the country streams.

I feared more than tigers their muscles like iron
Their jerking hands and their knees tight on my arms
I feared the salt coarse pointing of those boys
Who copied my lisp behind me on the road.

They were lithe they sprang out behind hedges
Like dogs to bark at my world. They threw mud
While I looked the other way, pretending to smile.
I longed to forgive them but they never smiled.

斯蒂芬·史彭德 / 作
Stephen Spender, 1909—1995
杨宪益 / 译

保姆之歌

草地上听到孩子们的声音,
山谷里也听到他们的细语轻声:
我年轻时的时日在我心上鲜明升起,
这时的我脸色苍白又发青。

那么回家吧,我的孩子们,日落了,
夜晚的露水将要出现,
你们的春天和白昼全浪费于玩耍,
你们的冬天和夜晚却是装假与欺骗。

Nurses Song

When the voices of children are heard on the green
And whisprings are in the dale:
The days of my youth rise fresh in my mind,
My face turns green and pale.

Then come home my children. the sun is gone down
And the dews of night arise
Your spring & your day. are wasted in play
And your winter and night in disguise.

威廉·布莱克/作
William Blake, 1757—1827
杨苡/译

扫烟囱的孩子

雪地里有一个黑黑的小东西,
叫喊着扫呀,扫呀,哭哭啼啼!
喂!你的爸爸妈妈都哪儿去了?
他们都到礼拜堂去做祷告。

因为我在荒原上本来很欢畅,
而且在冬天的大雪里微笑:
他们给我穿上了丧服似的衣裳。
又教我唱起这悲伤的曲调。

因为我快活,又跳又唱,
所以他们就以为对我毫无损伤:
就去赞美上帝与他的牧师和国王,
这一伙把我们的苦难硬说是天堂。

The Chimney Sweeper

A little black thing in the snow,
Crying "weep! weep!" in notes of woe!
"Where are thy father and mother? Say!"—
"They are both gone up to the church to pray.

"Because I was happy upon the heath,
And smiled among the winter's snow,
They clothed me in the clothes of death,
And taught me to sing the notes of woe.

"And because I am happy and dance and sing,
They think they have done me no injury,
And are gone to praise God and his priest and king,
Who make up a heaven of our misery."

威廉 · 布莱克 / 作
William Blake, 1757—1827
杨苡 / 译

流浪儿

亲爱的妈妈、亲爱的妈妈,教堂可真冷,
但酒店里却暖和,使人健康又开心,
而且我能知道在那儿过得好。
在天堂里我可绝没这么逍遥。

不过如果在教堂他们肯给我们点啤酒,
再给一炉旺火让我们的灵魂享受享受,
我们就会在漫长的日子里唱歌又祈祷,
也就一点不想离开教堂到处乱跑。

于是牧师就要祈祷,喝酒,又唱歌,
我们也会像春天里的鸟儿那样快乐,
而那位总是在教堂的文静的跛腿女先生,
就不会有弯腿的孩子、不禁食也不打人。

而上帝就像一个父亲,他高兴地看到,
他的孩子们都跟他一样地快乐逍遥,
也不会再跟魔鬼或酒鬼争吵个没完,
却是亲吻他,给他喝酒又给他衣服穿。

The Little Vagabond

Dear Mother, dear Mother, the Church is cold,
But the Ale-house is healthy & pleasant & warm;
Besides I can tell where I am use'd well,
Such usage in heaven will never do well.

But if at the Church they would give us some Ale.
And a pleasant fire, our souls to regale;
We'd sing and we'd pray, all the live-long day;
Nor ever once wish from the Church to stray,

Then the Parson might preach & drink & sing.
And we'd be as happy as birds in the spring:
And modest dame Lurch, who is always at Church,
Would not have bandy children nor fasting nor birch.

And God like a father rejoicing to see,
His children as pleasant and happy as he:
Would have no more quarrel with the Devil or the Barrel
But kiss him & give him both drink and apparel.

威廉·布莱克 / 作
William Blake, 1757—1827
杨苡 / 译

小学生

我爱在夏天清晨就起床,
当鸟儿在每一棵树上唱起歌。
远处的猎人把他的号角吹响,
而云雀在和我相互唱和。
哦!多么甜美的同伙。

可是夏天清早就上学堂,
哦!那就要驱散一切的欢乐;
忍受着凶狠的目光,
小家伙又叹气又难过,
就这样把日子消磨。

啊!那么我有时就垂头丧气地呆坐,
挨过了多少心神不定的时辰,
我既不能从书里得到快乐,
也不能稳坐学问的凉亭,
它已被阴郁的风雨磨损。

为欢乐而诞生的鸟儿又怎能
待在一只笼子里放声歌唱。
一个孩子当他胆战心惊
又怎能不耷拉他柔弱的翅膀,
并且把他的青春完全遗忘。

哦!父亲和母亲!

若花苞被摘掉，花朵全被吹散，
若柔弱的花木被夺去了
他们在萌芽时期的狂欢，
只由于愁哀与焦虑不安。

那么夏天将怎样欢快地升起，
夏天的果实又将怎样出现。
我们又将怎样把悲哀所毁坏的全部收集，
或怎样祝贺丰收的一年，
当冬天的风暴正在摧残。

The Schoolboy

I love to rise in a summer morn,
When the birds sing on every tree;
The distant huntsman winds his horn,
And the sky-lark sings with me.
O! what sweet company.

But to go to school in a summer morn,
O! it drives all joy away;
Under a cruel eye outworn.
The little ones spend the day,
In sighing and dismay.

Ah! then at times I drooping sit,
And spend many an anxious hour,
Nor in my book can I take delight,
Nor sit in learnings bower,
Worn thro' with the dreary shower.

How can the bird that is born for joy,
Sit in a cage and sing?
How can a child when fears and annoy,
But droop his tender wing,
And forget his youthful spring?

O! father & mother. if buds are nip'd,
And blossoms blown away,
And if the tender plants are strip'd
Of their joy in the springing day,
By sorrow and care's dismay.

How shall the summer arise in joy,
Or the summer fruits appear?
Or how shall we gather what griefs destroy,
Or bless the mellowing year,
When the blasts of winter appear?

威廉·布莱克 / 作
William Blake, 1757—1827
杨苡 / 译

一个小男孩的迷失

没有人爱别人像爱他自己,
也不会尊敬别人像对自己那样,
一个思想不可能去理解
另一个比它本身更伟大的思想。

天父啊,我怎么能对你,
或对任何我的兄弟爱得更深?
我爱你只能像那只小鸟儿,
在门边上把面包屑啄个不停。

坐在一旁的牧师听到孩子的话,
激动得直抖,抓住他的头发。
他拉着他的小衣裳、把他带走,
牧师的这份操心可让人人夸。

高高地站在圣坛上,他开口说:
瞧,这儿是个什么样的恶魔!
他竟敢批评我们最神圣的教义,
妄加推论全是一派胡说。

孩子的哭泣谁也听不见,
哭泣的父母白白地哭泣。
他们剥光他只剩一件小衬衫,
用一条铁链把他紧紧锁起。

在神圣的场所把他烧死,
以前那里也烧死过不少人。
哭泣的父母白白地哭泣,
这类事情是在不列颠海岸发生。

A Little Boy Lost

"Nought loves another as itself,
Nor venerates another so,
Nor is it possible to thought
A greater than itself to know.

"And, father, how can I love you
Or any of my brothers more?
I love you like the little bird
That picks up crumbs around the door."

The Priest sat by and heard the child;
In trembling zeal he seized his hair,
He led him by his little coat,
And all admired the priestly care.

And standing on the altar high,
"Lo, what a fiend is here! said he:
"One who sets reason up for judge
Of our most holy mystery."

The weeping child could not be heard,
The weeping parents wept in vain:
They stripped him to his little shirt,
And bound him in an iron chain,

And burned him in a holy place
Where many had been burned before;
The weeping parents wept in vain.
Are such thing done on Albion's shore?

威廉·布莱克 / 作
William Blake, 1757—1827
杨苡 / 译

一个小女孩的迷失

未来时代的孩子们，
读到这令人愤慨的一页，
知道了在从前有个时候
爱情！甜蜜的爱情！被当作是罪孽！

在黄金年代的时期，
没有冬日的寒冷天气，
活泼的少男少女，
在神圣的白昼里，
裸露在阳光下嬉戏。

有一次有一对年轻人
蕴藉着最温柔的关心，
在灿烂的花园里碰头，
那里神圣的白昼
刚把夜幕拉开没多久。

就在那里白日才升起，
他们在草地上嬉戏，
父亲和母亲离得还远，
陌生人也不会走近前，
姑娘不久就忘记她的不安。

亲吻又亲吻他们已很累，
他们约好何时再相会。

这时那默默的睡意朦胧,
飘过那深奥的天空,
而那疲乏的遨游者哀恸。

那活泼的少女
脸色发白到了父亲那里,
但是父亲的慈颜
就像那圣书一般,
她柔软的四肢吓得打颤。

欧娜苍白又软弱!
你要对你父亲直说:
哦,吓得直发抖!
哦,这凄凄惨惨的烦扰!
震撼着我的白发满头!

A Little Girl Lost

Children of the future age,
Reading this indignant page,
Know that in a former time
Love, sweet love, was thought a crime.

In the age of gold,
Free from winter's cold,
Youth and maiden bright,
To the holy light,
Naked in the sunny beams delight.

Once a youthful pair,
Filled with softest care,
Met in garden bright
Where the holy light
Had just removed the curtains of the night.

Then, in rising day,
On the grass they play;
Parents were afar,
Strangers came not near,
And the maiden soon forgot her fear.

Tired with kisses sweet,
They agree to meet
When the silent sleep
Waves o'er heaven's deep,
And the weary tired wanderers weep.

To her father white
Came the maiden bright;
But his loving look,
Like the holy book
All her tender limbs with terror shook.

"Ona, pale and weak,
To thy father speak!
Oh the trembling fear!
Oh the dismal care
That shakes the blossoms of my hoary hair!"

威廉·布莱克 / 作
William Blake, 1757—1827

杨苡 / 译

小女孩的迷失

在未来的时日
我预先看到,宛如先知,
大地从睡眠中苏醒。
(把这句话牢牢记在心。)

将起身去寻觅
她和善的上帝。
那一片荒凉的沙漠
将变成温暖的花园一座。

在南方的地区,
那里盛夏的时光,
永远不会消逝,
可爱的丽嘉躺卧在那里。

七个夏天已度过,
可爱的丽嘉说,
她一直在游荡,
听着那野鸟唱歌。

甜蜜的睡眠来找我吧
就在这棵树下。
爸爸妈妈会不会流泪——
"丽嘉能在哪儿安睡?"

你们的小孩子，
在荒凉的沙漠中迷失，
丽嘉怎么能安睡，
若是她妈妈在流泪。

若是妈妈在心疼，
那就让丽嘉仍清醒；
若是我的妈妈在安睡，
丽嘉也就不会流泪。

愁苦的愁苦的黑夜啊
笼罩着这明亮的荒野。
让你的月亮升起，
当我把我的眼睛紧闭。

当丽嘉躺卧着安眠，
从深深的山洞里面，
许多猛兽跑出来，
观察着这熟睡的女孩。

狮王站在那里
观察着这个童女，
然后他来回跳跃嬉戏，
在这块神圣的土地。

豹子、老虎也在玩耍，
就在她身边围绕。
这时那只年长的狮子

垂下它那一头金色的鬃毛,

便舔着她的胸膛,
它的眼睛灼灼有光,
流出红宝石般的眼泪,
滴落在她的颈项上;

这时母狮也来到身旁,
松开她纤细的衣裳,
它们把这熟睡的女孩
赤裸裸地搬到洞里来。

The Little Girl Lost

In futurity
I prophetic see,
That the earth from sleep.
(Grave the sentence deep)

Shall arise and seek
For her maker meek;
And the desart wild
Become a garden mild.

In the southern clime,
Where the summers prime,
Never fades away;
Lovely Lyca lay.

Seven summers old
Lovely Lyca told,
She had wandered long,
Hearing wild birds song.

Sweet sleep come to me
Underneath this tree;
Do father, mother weep-
"Where can Lyca sleep"?

Lost in desert wild
Is your little child.
How can Lyca sleep,
If her mother weep.

If her heart does ake,
Then let Lyca wake;

If my mother sleep,
Lyca shall not weep.

Frowning, frowning night,
O'er this desert bright,
Let thy moon arise,
While I close my eyes.

Sleeping Lyca lay;
While the beasts of prey,
Come from caverns deep,
View'd the maid asleep.

The kingly lion stood
And the virgin view'd,
Then he gambolled round
O'er the hallowed ground:

Leopards, tygers play,
Round her as she lay;
While the lion old,
Bow'd his mane of gold.

And her bosom lick,
And upon her neck,
From his eyes of flame
Ruby tears there came;

While the lioness
Loos'd her slender dress,
And naked they convey'd
To caves the sleeping maid.

威廉·布莱克 / 作
William Blake, 1757—1827

杨苡 / 译

小女孩的寻获

整个夜里在哭泣,
丽嘉的父母去寻觅,
越过幽深的溪谷,
沙漠也在啼哭。

他们伤心又疲乏,
声音也变哑,
手臂挽着手臂在这七天里,
在沙漠中追寻她的踪迹。

在这七天的夜里,
他们就在浓荫里憩息,
梦见了他们的孩子
在这荒凉的沙漠里饿死。

在没有人迹的道路上
那苍白的幻影在流浪,
饥饿又衰弱,正在哭泣,
夹杂着空洞的叫喊令人怜惜,

不能安宁只得起身,
这战栗的母亲又在前进,
一双脚又累又痛楚,
她已不能再迈一步。

他把她抱在怀里走,
抱着她,心里真难受。
走着走着竟然看见
一只狮子横躺在他们脚前。

他们来不及往回跑,
狮子重重的鬃毛,
将他们甩在地面,
然后阔步来回转。

嗅着它的捕获物,
但是他们的恐惧却止住,
当它舔着他们的手掌,
默默地站在他们身旁。

他们望着它的眼睛,
充满了深深的诧异的神情,
却又惊奇地看见,
一个金色披挂的小仙。

它头上戴一顶王冠,
它那金色的头发披散,
垂落在双肩。
这就消失了他们所有的焦念。

跟我来,它说,
不要为那姑娘难过。
在我幽静的宫殿里

丽嘉正在那里憩息。

然后他们跟随向前，
便目睹了这一个场面：
看见了他们熟睡的儿童
在那群野虎当中。

直到今天他们还留下住宿，
在一个僻静的小溪谷，
不怕豺狼的嚎叫，
也不怕狮子的咆哮。

The Little Girl Found

All the night in woe
Lyca's parents go
Over valleys deep,
While the deserts weep.

Tired and woe-begone,
Hoarse with making moan,
Arm in arm, seven days
They traced the desert ways.

Seven nights they sleep
Among shadows deep,
And dream they see their child
Starved in desert wild.

Pale through pathless ways
The fancied image strays,
Famished, weeping, weak,
With hollow piteous shriek.

Rising from unrest,
The trembling woman pressed
With feet of weary woe;
She could no further go.

In his arms he bore
Her, armed with sorrow sore;
Till before their way
A couching lion lay.

Turning back was vain:
Soon his heavy mane

Bore them to the ground,
Then he stalked around,

Smelling to his prey;
But their fears allay
When he licks their hands,
And silent by them stands.

They look upon his eyes,
Filled with deep surprise;
And wondering behold
A spirit armed in gold.

On his head a crown,
On his shoulders down
Flowed his golden hair.
Gone was all their care.

'Follow me,' he said;
'Weep not for the maid;
In my palace deep,
Lyca lies asleep.'

Then they followed
Where the vision led,
And saw their sleeping child
Among tigers wild.

To this day they dwell
In a lonely dell,
Nor fear the wolvish howl
Nor the lion's growl.

威廉·布莱克 / 作
William Blake, 1757—1827

杨苡 / 译

空洞的人

（过新年，喜事添，给社公社婆一个钱。）
一
我们是空洞的人，
我们是塞草的人。
倚在一起，
头上装满了干草。啊，
我们枯干的声音，
当我们一同私语，
是沉寂而无意义的，
有如风在枯死了的草间，
或老鼠的脚在碎玻璃上，
在我们干的酒窖里。

无形状的东西，无色彩的光影，
僵止的动力，无动作的形势。

那些已到了彼岸的人，
双目直视着，到了死的另一国土的，
记得我们。如果记得的话，不以我们为
流亡的猛厉的魂灵，只是
空洞的人，
塞草的人。

二
在梦里，我不敢遇见的眼睛，
在死的梦幻的国土里，

这些不出现。
在那里,眼睛是
一断柱上的阳光,
在那里,有树在摇动,
声音是
在风的歌里
比一残星,
更辽远幽肃。
让我不要更接近,
在死的梦幻的国土里。
让我也穿起,
如此故意的伪装,
老鼠的外衣,老鸦的皮,叉形的杖。
在一日里,
随风摇动着,
不更接近。

不要接近最后的会面,
在昏黄的国土里。

三

这是死的土地
这是不毛的土地。
在这里石像
森立,在这里,他们接受
一死人手的祈求,
在残星的闪光下。

是否如此,
在死的另一国土里?

独行踽踽,
当我们正为
温情而颤动,
将吻的唇
向断石祈祷。

四

那眼睛不在此处,
此处没有眼睛,
在这残星的谷里,
在这空洞的谷里,
我们失去国土的断颚。

在这最后会面的地方,
我们一同摸索着,
避免言语,
集合在这汹涌的河岸边。

看不见,除非
那眼睛再出现,
永久的星
发大光辉,升起,
从死的昏黄的国土里,
空洞的人的
希望。

五

在此处,我们绕着刺梨树,
刺梨树,刺梨树,
在此处,我们围绕着刺梨树,

在清晨五点钟的时候。

在观念
与现实之间,
在动作
与践行之间,
阴影降下了。
因为国土是你的。

在怀育
与创作之间,
在情感
与反应之间,
阴影降下了。
生命太长了。

在欲望
与满足之间,
在含蓄
与生存之间,
在原子
与降生之间,
阴影降下了。
因为国土是你的。
因为国土,
生命是,
因为国土是,
世界就如此终结,
世界就如此终结,
世界就如此终结,
不作大声,只作低声的怨泣。

The Hollow Men

I

We are the hollow men
We are the stuffed men
Leaning together
Headpiece filled with straw. Alas!
Our dried voices, when
We whisper together
Are quiet and meaningless
As wind in dry grass
Or rats' feet over broken glass
In our dry cellar

Shape without form, shade without colour,
Paralysed force, gesture without motion;

Those who have crossed
With direct eyes, to death's other Kingdom
Remember us — if at all — not as lost
Violent souls, but only
As the hollow men
The stuffed men.

II

Eyes I dare not meet in dreams
In death's dream kingdom
These do not appear:
There, the eyes are
Sunlight on a broken column
There, is a tree swinging

And voices are
In the wind's singing
More distant and more solemn
Than a fading star.

Let me be no nearer
In death's dream kingdom
Let me also wear
Such deliberate disguises
Rat's coat, crowskin, crossed staves
In a field
Behaving as the wind behaves
No nearer —

Not that final meeting
In the twilight kingdom

III

This is the dead land
This is cactus land
Here the stone images
Are raised, here they receive
The supplication of a dead man's hand
Under the twinkle of a fading star.

Is it like this
In death's other kingdom
Waking alone
At the hour when we are
Trembling with tenderness
Lips that would kiss
Form prayers to broken stone.

IV

The eyes are not here
There are no eyes here
In this valley of dying stars
In this hollow valley
This broken jaw of our lost kingdoms

In this last of meeting places
We grope together
And avoid speech
Gathered on this beach of the tumid river

Sightless, unless
The eyes reappear
As the perpetual star
Multifoliate rose
Of death's twilight kingdom
The hope only
Of empty men.

V

Here we go round the prickly pear
Prickly pear prickly pear
Here we go round the prickly pear
At five o'clock in the morning.

Between the idea
And the reality
Between the motion
And the act
Falls the Shadow

For Thine is the Kingdom
Between the conception
And the creation
Between the emotion

And the response
Falls the Shadow
Life is very long

Between the desire
And the spasm
Between the potency
And the existence
Between the essence
And the descent
Falls the Shadow
For Thine is the Kingdom
For Thine is
Life is
For Thine is the
This is the way the world ends
This is the way the world ends
This is the way the world ends
Not with a bang but a whimper.

T. S. 艾略特 / 作
T. S. Eliot, 1888—1965
杨宪益 / 译

苦行者

苦行者站在柱顶,
只有一个孤柱。
他已站立了这许久,
身体变成石铸。
只有他的眼睛还
远远望着大荒,
那里从没有人来,
世界一片茫茫。

他闭上他的眼睛,
梦里还是站着。
在他头颈的四围,
有绳子的感觉。
刽子手正在数着,
从一要数到十。
数到九他又觉得,
眼睛没有化石。

苦行者站在柱顶,
石柱有了两个,
一青年人在空中,
站在他的对过,
雪白的希腊神像,
充满自信骄态。
鬈发站在屋棱上,
双眼看着世界。

Stylite

The saint on the pillar stands,
The pillar is alone,
He has stood so long
That he himself is stone;
Only his eyes
Range across the sand
Where no one ever comes
And the world is banned.

Then his eyes close
He stands in his sleep,
Round his neck there comes
The conscience of a rope,
And the hangman counting
Counting to ten—
At nine he finds
He has eyes again.

The saint on the pillar stands,
The pillars are two,
A young man opposite
Stands in the blue,
A white Greek god,
Confident, with curled
Hair above the groin
And his eyes on the world.

路易斯·麦克尼斯 / 作
Louis MacNeice, 1907—1963
杨宪益 / 译

雪岭上的苦行人

文化是被多端的幻觉圈起,
在一定范围内,和平的外表下。
但人的生命是思想,虽恐怕
也必须追求,经过无数世纪,
追求着,狂索着,摧毁着,他要
最后能来到那现实的荒野。
别了,埃及和希腊,别了,罗马。
苦行人在金山雪岭上修道,
深夜时,在山窟中,在积雪底,
或雪与寒风击他们的裸体,
知白昼带来夜,在破晓时候,
他的乐观与华炫将成乌有。

(英文版本未找到)

W. B. 叶芝 / 作
W. B. Yeats, 1865—1939

杨宪益 / 译

古行吟诗人的声音

快乐的青年，到这里来，
来看这正在展示的曙光，
是新生真理的意象，
疑虑已溜走，理智的乌云，
阴郁的争论，狡狯的嘲弄全逃遁。
愚蠢是一条无穷尽的曲径。
盘曲的树根使道路艰险难行，
有多少人在那里跌倒！
他们整夜在死人的骸骨上蹒跚前行，
还觉得他们想知道的全知道，
还想带领人当他们还要人带领。

The Voice of the Ancient Bard

Youth of delight, come hither,
And see the opening morn,
Image of truth new born.
Doubt is fled, & clouds of reason,
Dark disputes & artful teazing.
Folly is an endless maze,
Tangled roots perplex her ways.
How many have fallen there!
They stumble all night over bones of the dead,
And feel they know not what but care,
And wish to lead others, when they should be led.

威廉·布莱克 / 作
William Blake, 1757—1827

杨苡 / 译

我已故的公爵夫人

在墙壁上画的是我已故的公爵夫人,
看起来好像她还是活着的。如今我称
那幅画是一件珍品:潘道夫教兄的手
苦干了一整天,这样她就伫立在那头。
请你坐下来看看她好么?我有意提起
是潘道夫教兄画的,因为像你这样的
生人可从来没有见过那画上的面容,
那热诚的顾盼中露出的深意与热情,
但他们总要转身问我(还没有哪一个
拉开我刚才为你拉开的幔帐,除了我)
而且看来他们想问我,如果他们敢问,
怎么有这样的眼色,所以,并非第一人
像你转过身来这样问。先生,这并不是
仅仅有她的丈夫在身旁时,才会招致
那红晕现在公爵夫人的脸上,说不定
潘道夫教兄偶尔碰巧说:"夫人的披风
遮盖夫人的手腕太多了",或者说"描绘
决不要指望可以复制出那一种轻微
羞涩的红晕消失在喉头。"这胡言乱语
是殷勤好意的,她以为,这就足以招致
那一片表示欢喜的红晕。她有一颗心,
叫我怎么说呢?很快就可以让她高兴,
太容易受感动了,她是见了什么都喜欢,
而且她还到处无论什么都想看一看。
先生,什么都一样!我给她胸饰的礼品,
黄昏时分夕阳西下白昼渐渐地下沉,

挂满了樱桃的树枝，有些多事的笨伯
为了她在果园里把它折断，那匹白骡
它绕着庭院驰骋——一切一切，每一件事
都会从她嘴里引出类似的赞许言词，
或至少脸红。她向人道谢——好呀！可那样
道谢的神气，我说不出怎样，就像是她将
我赠与她的九百年悠久的名门显赫
同任何人的礼物并列。谁屈就去指责
这一类琐碎事呢？即使是你有这本事
精于谈吐（我可是没有的），把你的意思
对这么个人说清楚，就说："就是这件事
或那件你使我厌烦，这儿你有过失
或那儿你有过分。"而如果她就让自己
全听从你这样的教诲，也不坦率地
和你斗智，真是的，还找借口狂费口舌，
即使是那样也是有点屈就，我就选择
决不屈就。噢，先生，她微笑着，毫无疑问
任何时候我走过她身边，但哪一个人
走过没有同样笑？这样下去，我就下令，
于是所有的笑全停了。她在那里站定
像还活着。请你起来好吗？我们要见见
楼下一群朋友们。我还要重复一遍。
令东家，伯爵大人素以乐善好施著称，
这就是以保证我的正当要求来联姻，
他总不会不答应给我我索取的妆奁
虽然他漂亮的女儿本人，我声明在先，
那才是我追求的目的。不谈这些，我们
一块下楼去吧，先生。可是，瞧瞧那海神
驯服一匹海马，被人当做一件珍品呢，
是因斯勒的克劳斯为我用青铜雕的。

My Last Duchess

That's my last Duchess painted on the wall,
Looking as if she were alive. I call
That piece a wonder, now; Fra Pandolf's hands
Worked busily a day, and there she stands.
Will't please you sit and look at her? I said
"Fra Pandolf" by design, for never read
Strangers like you that pictured countenance,
The depth and passion of its earnest glance,
But to myself they turned (since none puts by
The curtain I have drawn for you, but I)
And seemed as they would ask me, if they durst,
How such a glance came there; so, not the first
Are you to turn and ask thus. Sir, 'twas not
Her husband's presence only, called that spot
Of joy into the Duchess' cheek; perhaps
Fra Pandolf chanced to say, "Her mantle laps
Over my lady's wrist too much," or "Paint
Must never hope to reproduce the faint
Half-flush that dies along her throat." Such stuff
Was courtesy, she thought, and cause enough
For calling up that spot of joy. She had
A heart—how shall I say?— too soon made glad,
Too easily impressed; she liked whate'er
She looked on, and her looks went everywhere.
Sir, 'twas all one! My favour at her breast,
The dropping of the daylight in the West,
The bough of cherries some officious fool
Broke in the orchard for her, the white mule
She rode with round the terrace—all and each

Would draw from her alike the approving speech,
Or blush, at least. She thanked men—good! but thanked
Somehow—I know not how—as if she ranked
My gift of a nine-hundred-years-old name
With anybody's gift. Who'd stoop to blame
This sort of trifling? Even had you skill
In speech—which I have not—to make your will
Quite clear to such an one, and say, "Just this
Or that in you disgusts me; here you miss,
Or there exceed the mark"—and if she let
Herself be lessoned so, nor plainly set
Her wits to yours, forsooth, and made excuse—
E'en then would be some stooping; and I choose
Never to stoop. Oh, sir, she smiled, no doubt,
Whene'er I passed her; but who passed without
Much the same smile? This grew; I gave commands;
Then all smiles stopped together. There she stands
As if alive. Will't please you rise? We'll meet
The company below, then. I repeat,
The Count your master's known munificence
Is ample warrant that no just pretense
Of mine for dowry will be disallowed;
Though his fair daughter's self, as I avowed
At starting, is my object. Nay, we'll go
Together down, sir. Notice Neptune, though,
Taming a sea-horse, thought a rarity,
Which Claus of Innsbruck cast in bronze for me!

罗伯特·勃朗宁 / 作
Robert Browning, 1812—1889

杨苡 / 译

列宁

如此我下了台阶，来见列宁。
有一群的农夫在我面前，
和我的后面。我就看见了
一间涂红的屋子。那里有
一矮小蜡人在玻璃匣里。
足前两个兵，一个在头边。
细弱的双手，放在他胸前，
如虔诚的处女安眠。我说，
这双手曾发布许多命令。
四围有光辉，在他赤发上。
他还是穿着他的旧制服。
贪看得仔细，我就又看到，
在这限定的两分钟里面，
他不是蜡的，如他们所说，
是肉体，因为指甲是黑的。
这就是列宁。
那时一妇人在我旁呼喊，
用一高亢的异国的语言。
我向不怕生与死，只略怕
死人，心中忽为恐惧震撼。
因为我站在上帝的面前，
我听的声音，是历代语言，
迎新的可怖的美的信仰。
我知她哭泣，如古人哭泣，
为基督被放在坟墓里面。
基督也是一个蜡做的人，
当他们送他入土的时候。

From "Lenin"

So I came down the steps to Lenin.
With a herd of peasants before
And behind me, I saw
A room stained scarlet, and there
A small wax man in a small glass case.
Two sentinels at his feet, and one at his head,
Two little hands on his breast:
Pious spinster asleep; and I said
'Many warrants these delicate hands have signed.'
A lamp shone, red,
An aureole over him, on his red hair;
His uniform clothed him still.
Greedy of detail I saw,
In those two minutes allowed,
The man was not wax, as they said,
But a corpse, for a thumb nail was black,
The thing was Lenin.
Then a woman beside me cried
With a strange voice, foreign, loud.
And I, who fear not life nor death, and those who have died
Only a little, was inwardly shaken with fear,
For I stood in the presence of God;
The voice I heard was the voice of all generations
Acclaiming new faiths, horrible, beautiful faiths;
I knew that the woman wailed as women wailed long ago
For Christ in the sepulchre laid.
Christ was a wax man too,
When they carried Him down to the grave.

多萝西·韦尔斯利 / 作
Dorothy Wellesley, 1889—1956

杨宪益 / 译

梭罗门与巫女

那天方的巫女如此发言,
"昨夜在荒凉的月色下面,
我正倦卧在蔓草的茵上,
在我怀中睡着梭罗门王,
我忽然发出奇异的喋喋,
非人类语言。"他因能了解
一切飞鸟,或天使的歌声,
就说,"一锦冠的鹦鹉,也曾
在繁华的苹果树上歌啼,
失乐园前三百年的时期。
从那时到现在,就没有唱。
其实本不当唱,可是它想,
'故意'与'偶然'又遇在一处。
那苹果带来的一切痛苦
和这坏的世界,终于死去。
它曾把'永恒'在过去叫走,
以为现在又把它叫回头。
爱恋着的人有蜘蛛的眼,
虽然他眼里充满了爱恋,
每一神经都充满,但这两人
还以'故意'和'偶然'的残忍,
来彼此试探。虽两败俱伤,
新婚的床上又带来失望。
因每人都有幻想的形象,
而终发觉了那真的模样。

'故意'和'偶然'二物虽不同，
但为一体时，世界就告终。
当油与灯芯，焚在一火中。
所以昨天夜里，明月多情，
使巫女西跋见了梭罗门。"
"但世界还存在"，"若是如此，
你的鹦鹉做了一件错事。
可是它想值得它叫一次。
也许那个幻想有如实有，
也许那个幻象像得不够。"
"夜色降下了。也没有声息
在这不可侵犯的灵薮里，
除去有花蕊落地的细声，
在这灵薮里，也没有旁人，
只有我们所卧蔓草的茵。
月色也渐变神异而荒凉。
好不好再试试？梭罗门王？"

Solomon And The Witch

And thus declared that Arab lady:
'Last night, where under the wild moon
On grassy mattress I had laid me,
Within my arms great Solomon,
I suddenly cried out in a strange tongue
Not his, not mine.'
Who understood
Whatever has been said, sighed, sung,
Howled, miau-d, barked, brayed, belled, yelled, cried, crowed,
Thereon replied: 'A cockerel
Crew from a blossoming apple bough
Three hundred years before the Fall,
And never crew again till now,
And would not now but that he thought,
Chance being at one with Choice at last,
All that the brigand apple brought
And this foul world were dead at last.
He that crowed out eternity
Thought to have crowed it in again.
For though love has a spider's eye
To find out some appropriate pain –
Aye, though all passion's in the glance –
For every nerve, and tests a lover
With cruelties of Choice and Chance;
And when at last that murder's over
Maybe the bride-bed brings despair,
For each an imagined image brings
And finds a real image there;
Yet the world ends when these two things,

Though several, are a single light,
When oil and wick are burned in one;
Therefore a blessed moon last night
Gave Sheba to her Solomon.'
'Yet the world stays.'
'If that be so,
Your cockerel found us in the wrong
Although he thought it. worth a crow.
Maybe an image is too strong
Or maybe is not strong enough.'
'The night has fallen; not a sound
In the forbidden sacred grove
Unless a petal hit the ground,
Nor any human sight within it
But the crushed grass where we have lain!
And the moon is wilder every minute.
O! Solomon! let us try again.'

W. B. 叶茨 / 作
W. B. Yeats, 1865—1939

杨宪益 / 译

辑四

我一下子跳进这危险的世界:无依无靠,光着身,尖声喊叫,就像躲在云彩里的一个魔妖。
——《婴儿的悲哀》

诞辰

我的心像一只歌唱着的鸟,
它的巢筑在水边的嫩枝间;
我的心像是一棵苹果树,
它的枝已被累累果实压弯;
我的心像一架彩虹的桥影,
浮在一片翡翠的海中摇摆。
我的心比这一切都更欢欣,
因为我的爱已经向我走来。

给我挂起一台丝绒织的毯,
缀上松鼠皮,并且染上紫色,
再刻上些鸽子,还有石榴树,
还要有一百只眼睛的孔雀;
织上金色的和银色的葡萄,
叶子和银色的鸢尾花盛开。
因为我生命的诞辰已来到,
我的爱已经,已经向我走来。

A Birthday

My heart is like a singing bird
Whose nest is in a water'd shoot;
My heart is like an apple-tree
Whose boughs are bent with thickset fruit;
My heart is like a rainbow shell
That paddles in a halcyon sea;
My heart is gladder than all these
Because my love is come to me.

Raise me a dais of silk and down;
Hang it with vair and purple dyes;
Carve it in doves and pomegranates,
And peacocks with a hundred eyes;
Work it in gold and silver grapes,
In leaves and silver fleurs-de-lys;
Because the birthday of my life
Is come, my love is come to me.

克里斯汀娜·罗塞蒂 / 作
Christina Rossetti, 1830—1894
杨苡 / 译

婴儿的悲哀

我妈妈呻吟！我爸爸流泪。
我一下子跳进这危险的世界：
无依无靠，光着身，尖声喊叫，
就像躲在云彩里的一个魔妖。

我在爸爸的手里拼命挣脱，
就想蹬掉束缚我的那堆包裹：
使我动不了，还很疲劳，
还不如索性躺在妈妈的怀抱。

Infant Sorrow

My mother groaned, my father wept,
Into the dangerous world I leapt;
Helpless, naked, piping loud,
Like a fiend hid in a cloud.

Struggling in my father's hands,
Striving against my swaddling bands,
Bound and weary, I thought best
To sulk upon my mother's breast.

威廉·布莱克 / 作
William Blake, 1757—1827

杨苡 / 译

五月

我不能告诉你是怎么回事,
我只知道这个:它已经过去,
在一个晴朗有微风的日子。
五月正年轻,啊,欢悦的时日,
那些罂粟花都还没有茁生,
在那纤细的嫩叶丛的当中
最后的一批卵还没有孵出,
也没有鸟儿离开它的伴侣。

我不能告诉你是怎么回事,
我只知道这个:它已经过去。
它同灿烂的五月一同去了,
带着所有的甜蜜它消逝了,
丢下我老了,冷了,而且灰了。

May

I cannot tell you how it was,
But this I know: it came to pass
Upon a bright and sunny day
When May was young; ah, pleasant May!
As yet the poppies were not born
Between the blades of tender corn;
The last egg had not hatched as yet,
Nor any bird foregone its mate.

I cannot tell you what it was,
But this I know: it did but pass.
It passed away with sunny May,
Like all sweet things it passed away,
And left me old, and cold, and gray.

克里斯汀娜·罗塞蒂 / 作
Christina Rossetti, 1830—1894

杨苡 / 译

空袭

是的,我们将遭受苦难了,天
悸动如狂热的额。真的痛苦。
摸索着的探照灯光,忽显出
卑微的人性,使得我们乞怜。

因它们存在,我们向未相信,
这里它们突然使我们惊异,
如丑恶的久忘记了的记忆,
而如良心责备,一切炮回应。

每一双和易的眼睛的后背,
都有暗地的屠杀在进行中,
一切妇女,犹太人,富人,人类。

高山不能判断匍匐的我们,
我们住在地上,大地总服从
狡恶的人们,除非人不生存。

Sonnets from China - 14 (XIV)

Yes, we are going to suffer, now; the sky
Throbs like a feverish forehead; pain is real;
The groping searchlights suddenly reveal
The little natures that will make us cry,

Who never quite believed they could exist,
Not where we were. They take us by surprise
Like ugly long-forgotten memories,
And like a conscience all the guns resist.

Behind each sociable home-loving eye
The private massacres are taking place;
All Women, Jews, the Rich, the Human Race.

The mountains cannot judge us when we lie:
We dwell upon the earth; the earth obeys
The intelligent and evil till they die.

W. H. 奥登 / 作
W. H. Auden, 1907—1973

杨宪益 / 译

爱尔兰空军驾驶员

我知道我的生命将结束,
在天上某处,在云层以外。
我所攻击的人我并不恨,
我所护卫的人我也不爱。
我的家乡是吉尔塔坦村,
我的亲友是那里的穷人。
结果怎样他们总无所损,
他们也不会比以前欢欣。
不是法律、义务,使我参战,
不是红会人物,不是民众。
一时忽然觉得很好玩,
激起我到云层间去活动。
我想过一切,都计算好了,
未来的生活也必是白忙,
过去的岁月也更是无聊。
这个死同这个生活一样。

An Irish Airman Forsees His Death

I know that I shall meet my fate
Somewhere among the clouds above;
Those that I fight I do not hate,
Those that I guard I do not love;
My county is Kiltartan Cross,
My countrymen Kiltartan's poor,
No likely end could bring them loss
Or leave them happier than before.
Nor law, nor duty bade me fight,
Nor public men, nor cheering crowds,
A lonely impulse of delight
Drove to this tumult in the clouds;
I balanced all, brought all to mind,
The years to come seemed waste of breath,
A waste of breath the years behind
In balance with this life, this death.

W. B. 叶茨 / 作
W. B. Yeats, 1865—1939

杨宪益 / 译

暴露

我们脑筋痛,在刺人的东风里。
疲倦,我们醒着,因为夜太沉默。
低落照明弹,紊乱阵线的记忆。
忧郁的步哨私语着,怀疑不安。
可是前线还是无事。

注视着,我们听狂风摇着铁网,
有如痉挛苦痛的人,在荆棘中。
在北方,不停的内火的炮轰击,
遥远如另一战争隐隐的谣言。
我们在这里做什么?

晨光刺目的痛苦,渐渐增高了,
战争还继续着,雨浸着,云垂着。
在东方,晨光列成愁郁的阵容,
又对战栗的灰色的行列总攻。
可是前线还是无事。

忽然子弹继续飞来,经过沉默,
还不如那雪凝阴冷的天厉害。
斜飞的雪花,成群的停顿,继续,
它们在风里随意的上下飘游。
可是前线还是无事。

雪花灰白,偷偷来触我们的脸。
我们畏缩,回想旧梦,直视,昏眩。
伸缩在有草的战壕里,假寐着,
如有缤纷的花,乱叫的白头翁。
我们是不是将死了。

慢慢的魂回家,瞥见将灭的火,
有残烬点缀。蟋蜂在那里鸣着。
老鼠们嬉戏着,房子是它们的。
门窗都关起,把我们关在外面。
魂回到将死的身体。

因相信这样,才有温和的炉火,
才有阳光,在幼儿、田地、果实上。
我们怕上帝所赐的春天死去,
所以卧待不怨,所以生在世上。
因上帝的爱要死了。

今夜严霜将降在我们的面上,
使许多人的手与额冻僵,皱缩。
埋尸首的人,手里拿着锄和铲,
经过旧识的脸,暂停,眼结成冰。
可是前线还是无事。

Exposure

Our brains ache, in the merciless iced east winds that knive us...
Wearied we keep awake because the night is silent...
Low drooping flares confuse our memory of the salient...
Worried by silence, sentries whisper, curious, nervous,
But nothing happens.

Watching, we hear the mad gusts tugging on the wire,
Like twitching agonies of men among its brambles.
Northward, incessantly, the flickering gunnery rumbles,
Far off, like a dull rumour of some other war.
What are we doing here?

The poignant misery of dawn begins to grow...
We only know war lasts, rain soaks, and clouds sag stormy.
Dawn massing in the east her melancholy army
Attacks once more in ranks on shivering ranks of grey,
But nothing happens.

Sudden successive flights of bullets streak the silence.
Less deadly than the air that shudders black with snow,
With sidelong flowing flakes that flock, pause, and renew,
We watch them wandering up and down the wind's nonchalance,
But nothing happens.

Pale flakes with fingering stealth come feeling for our faces—
We cringe in holes, back on forgotten dreams, and stare, snow-dazed,
Deep into grassier ditches. So we drowse, sun-dozed,
Littered with blossoms trickling where the blackbird fusses.
—Is it that we are dying?

Slowly our ghosts drag home: glimpsing the sunk fires, glozed
With crusted dark-red jewels; crickets jingle there;
For hours the innocent mice rejoice: the house is theirs;
Shutters and doors, all closed: on us the doors are closed,
—We turn back to our dying.

Since we believe not otherwise can kind fires burn;
Now ever suns smile true on child, or field, or fruit.
For God's invincible spring our love is made afraid;
Therefore, not loath, we lie out here; therefore were born,
For love of God seems dying.

Tonight, this frost will fasten on this mud and us,
Shrivelling many hands, and puckering foreheads crisp.
The burying-party, picks and shovels in shaking grasp,
Pause over half-known faces. All their eyes are ice,
But nothing happens.

威尔弗雷德·欧文 / 作
Wilfred Owen, 1893—1918

杨宪益 / 译

飞天夜叉（空袭后写成）

一

在有雾的夜里，如白痴一般哼着，
它们在屋顶上徘徊，咕噜，蹒跚，踉跄，
从广厦到高柱，穿着碾碎星的重靴，
脸上带着死板板的痴笑，
有千人针总死不了。
粗鲁的嬉戏，古怪的声音，它们不知道做的什么事。
它们只知道吃吃地摆动，骑着鬼马，压
它们靴底的铁钉，到我们身体里，到我们脑筋里，
到有圣乐摇曳的教堂的圆顶里，
有千人针总死不了。
它们来了，我以为找不到它们了，
它们又来了，又来的不少，来玩它们粗鲁的
把戏，它们
来了，来了，来了！
有千人针总死不了。
死不了？

二

没有比这不同的，
此外什么都不应当有，
这就是它们所说的生活。
这样咕噜着，践踏着，吃着手指头，在它们
翻过这一页，撕去这一页之前，它们
希望我们消灭，它们
鼓着嘴吹，这太空中的一羽，

勾销了时刻。

三

死是含有决定的意味的。
我们以为我们失去了什么,可是如没有
死,我们也就无物可失。无限制的
生存,也就成为非具体的
生存,夜叉能使
我们死,可是它们不能
利用死,如我们一样。
摸索着,喃喃地说着,它们要
我们死灭,它们做不到!

四

此外没有别的,时间
在死的两极间颤动,
而生命的经纬
都已死为终限。每一个
机构,行动,与时间的价值,
都是因了死,而有了特殊的意义。

五

这就是我们在这劫火飞落里的答复。
我们最后还握着拳,
反抗那渐渐看不见了的天空,
反抗那些笨重的疯癫的怪物,
它们行着强暴,流着馋涎,以为
把我们弄死,就再没有别的。
人类的永默,夜叉的胜利。
一个终于是错误的估计。
在天上推着,挤着,一群废物

糊涂地滚下来,
它们打算要把人的声音永远取消,
可是它们要做的,
是就连夜叉也做不到的事。
它们总是,
虽然有这么大的威风,
但错了。终究是错了。

(英文版本未找到)

路易斯·麦克尼斯 / 作
Louis MacNeice, 1907—1963

杨宪益 / 译

回营时听见天鹅的歌声

夜色是阴沉的,
我们虽保留了性命,我们知道
那里还藏着不祥的恫吓。

拖着我们苦痛的身体,我们只知道
这被毒气摧残的路,直达我们的营,
和短促的安眠。

可是听,欢乐啊,奇异的欢乐啊!
在夜色的高处,有看不见的天鹅歌唱,
乐音降落到我们仰着静听的脸上。

死亡也能从黑暗中降下,
如同歌声一样容易,
可是只有歌声降下了。
如盲人的梦在沙滩上,
在危险的潮汐边,
如少女的黑发,因她想不到里面有人的灾祸,
或她藏着毒蛇的吻。

Returning, We Hear the Larks

Sombre the night is:
And, though we have our lives, we know
What sinister threat lurks there.

Dragging these anguished limbs, we only know
This poison-blasted track opens on our camp—
On a little safe sleep.

But hark! Joy—joy—strange joy.
Lo! Heights of night ringing with unseen larks:
Music showering on our upturned listening faces.

Death could drop from the dark
As easily as song—
But song only dropped,
Like a blind man's dreams on the sand
By dangerous tides;
Like a girl's dark hair, for she dreams no ruin lies there,
Or her kisses where a serpent hides.

艾萨克·罗森堡 / 作
Isaac Rosenberg, 1890—1918

杨宪益 / 译

资本家最后的统治方法

机枪以铅铸的字,在春天山边,
发出资本家最后的统治方法。
可是这孩子死在橄榄树下的,
是太年轻,太单纯了,而不敢当
这些大人物的眼,来加以注意。
(他应该是吻),不是枪弹的目标。

高耸的工场汽笛尚未招呼他,
旅馆的玻璃转门尚未欢迎他,
他的名字永未在报纸上见过,
这世界保持它那传统的高墙,
在那些深藏金钱的死者四围。
他在墙外飘荡虚幻有如谣言。

啊,他掷下的小帽,太随便了,
那正是微风吹落花蕊的一天,
这不开花的墙忽生满了枪支,
怒吼的机枪疾速地切断了草,
从手中、枝上,旗帜与树叶落下,
毛织的小帽就在荆棘间朽烂。

你想一想,他的生命,是不值钱,
在职业、账目、档案等方面来看。
一万子弹里只有一个打死人。
你说,这许多费用是否值得?
为一个如此年轻而单纯的人,
死在橄榄树下?啊,世界啊,死亡。

Ultima Ratio Regum

The guns spell money's ultimate reason
In letters of lead on the spring hillside.
But the boy lying dead under the olive trees
Was too young and too silly
To have been notable to their important eye.
He was a better target for a kiss.

When he lived, tall factory hooters never summoned him.
Nor did restaurant plate-glass doors revolve to wave him in.
His name never appeared in the papers.
The world maintained its traditional wall
Round the dead with their gold sunk deep as a well,
Whilst his life, intangible as a Stock Exchange rumour, drifted outside.

O too lightly he threw down his cap
One day when the breeze threw petals from the trees.
The unflowering wall sprouted with guns,
Machine-gun anger quickly scythed the grasses;
Flags and leaves fell from hands and branches;
The tweed cap rotted in the nettles.

Consider his life which was valueless
In terms of employment, hotel ledgers, news files.
Consider. One bullet in ten thousand kills a man.
Ask. Was so much expenditure justified
On the death of one so young and so silly
Lying under the olive tree, O world, O death?

斯蒂芬·史彭德 / 作
Stephen Spender, 1909—1995

杨宪益 / 译

孩子们的哭声

一

你有没有听见孩子们在哭泣,啊,我的兄弟们,
就在岁月还不该带来悲哀的时候?
他们将他们幼小的头颅靠着他们的母亲,
可那也不能阻挡他们的泪水直流。
小羊在草地上咩咩啼,
小鸟在窝里叫唧唧,
小鹿在和影子嬉戏,
小花被风吹向西,
可是幼小的、幼小的孩子们啊,我的兄弟们,
他们还在苦苦地哭泣!
他们哭泣在别的孩子们玩耍的时辰,
在这自由人民的国度里。①

二

你有没有询问那些悲哀的孩子们,
他们的眼泪为什么这样直流?
老人会为他们的明天哭泣,
这个明天早已失去很久,很久。
古老的树在森林中落尽树叶,
往昔的岁月在严寒中完结,
以前的创伤,要是碰一下,会痛得最剧烈,
旧日的希望是最难以被人忘却,

---

① 英国当时号称"大不列颠,自由人民的土地"。

可是幼小的、幼小的孩子们,啊,我的兄弟们,
你有没有问他们为什么站在那里,
在他们的母亲的胸前痛哭失声,
在我们这幸福美满的祖国大地?

三

他们仰起苍白瘦削的脸,
他们的神色令人悲哀,
因为成人的忧伤竟然
在这些幼儿的脸上刻划出来。
"你这古老的大地,"他们说,"十分凄惨。"
"我们的小脚,"他们说,"软弱无力。"
"我们还没走几步,却已疲倦——
让我们休息的坟墓又是远得没法寻觅。
问问那些年老的人他们为什么哭泣,别问我,
因为外面的大地冰冷,
而我们幼小的人站在外面,手足无措,
坟墓却仅仅是为了年老的人。"

四

"真的,"幼小的孩子们说,"说不定
我们就会碰巧短寿。
小爱丽丝去年死掉——那座坟
被白霜遮盖,就像一个雪球。
我们望着那准备收容她的坟墓坑——
在封闭的泥巴里可没有干活的地方。
谁也不会把她从睡眠中唤醒,
叫着,'起来吧,小爱丽丝,天已大亮。'

如果你在那座坟旁留神听,无论天晴或下雨,
你用耳俯听,小爱丽丝决不会哭叫!
要是我们能看见她的脸,一定会不认识,
因为在她的眼里居然可以现出微笑。
她的时光过得多么快活,被尸衣包裹,
教堂的钟声在催她安眠!"
"那有多好,"孩子们说,
"要是我们的死期也能提前。"①

五

天哪,天哪。孩子们他们还活着
却寻求死亡,说是最好是死去!
他们从坟墓里取出一块裹尸布,
围住他们的心以防破裂。
走出去吧,孩子们,从矿井和城市走开。
放声唱吧,孩子们,像小画眉鸣叫。
把那漂亮的樱草花大量地摘采,
大声笑吧,来感觉花儿在你手指间穿绕!
然而他们回答,"你那草地上的樱草花
像不像矿井附近我们那堆杂草?
让我们安静地在煤影的黑暗中待着吧,
去你的那些漂亮美好的愉快逍遥!"

六

"因为啊,"孩子们说,"我们很累,
我们跑不动也没法跳。
如果我们巴望什么草地,也无非

---

① 这首诗每段十二行,唯独本段十六行。

想倒在那儿好睡个觉。

我们的膝盖一蹲下就发颤，

我们的脸朝下扑倒，又勉强爬起来，

而在我们沉重的耷拉着的眼皮下面，

最红的花儿也像是雪一样地苍白，

因为一整天我们拖着我们累人的重担，

穿过地底下，黢黑黢黑，

或者一整天我们推着那些铁轮到处转，

在那些工厂里，转去又转回。"

七

"因为一整天轮子在转着嗡嗡响，

它扇出的风扑向我们的脸，

直到我们的心也在转，我们的头、脉搏也烫，

墙壁也在它的原地打转，

天空在高高的摇晃着的窗框中打转，

沿着墙壁垂下的长长的光线打转，

顺着天花板爬着的黑苍蝇打转——

一切在打转，整天，我们和一切都在转。

而一整天，铁轮单调地发出嗡嗡声，

有时候我们也会祷告，

'啊，你们这些轮子啊，'（迸发出疯狂的呻吟）

'停停吧！今天就安静一下好不好？'"

八

喂，安静！就让他们听一听

彼此的呼吸，嘴对着嘴。

让他们摸到彼此的手，沉浸

在他们那温柔的人类青春旺盛的氛围！
让他们认为这冰冷的金属运转，
并不是上帝缔造或启示的生命的全部，
让他们证明他们的心灵反对这个概念，
说他们活在你里面，或在你下面，啊，轮子！
仍然在转，一整天，铁轮向前滚，
从生命的起点就开始将生命细碾，
而上帝在召唤向着太阳的孩子们的灵魂，
却盲目地在黑暗中继续旋转。

九

现在，告诉那些可怜的小孩子，啊，我的兄弟们！
要仰望他，并且祈求，
这样那位保佑所有别人的降福之神，
才会也有一天将他保佑。
他们回答："该听到我们祈求的那位上帝是谁，
当铁轮横冲直撞，乱哄哄地响？
当我们高声抽泣，那些挨近我们的人类
却走过，根本不听，一个字也不搭腔！
而我们也听不见(因为轮子在轰响)。
在门外说话的陌生人，
是不是像个上帝，有天使在他周围歌唱，
是否还能再听见我们的哭声？

十

"的确，我们只记得祷告中的两个字，
而且是在半夜里发生不幸的时辰，
'天父'，我们在屋里仰望注视，

轻声要求有一道符咒来护身。
我们除了'天父',并不知道别的字,
我们以为趁着天使的歌唱偶尔停顿,
上帝就会以甜蜜的沉默将祷告收集起,
并且把这两个字抓在他的强有力的右手中。
'天父',如果他听见了我们,他一定会
(因为他们说他又善良又和气)
十分纯洁地微笑着俯视这不合理的世界,
回答说,'我的孩子,来和我一起休息。'"

十一

"可是不,"孩子们说,哭得更响,
"他像块石头似的不吭声,
而他们告诉我们,关于他的形象
就像命令我们不停干活的那个主人。"
"去吧!"孩子们说,"在天堂中,
我们找到的也只是像轮子的乌云在打转。
别嘲笑我们,悲哀已使我们不能相信——
我们仰望上帝,但泪水已使我们看不见。"
你有没有听见孩子们哭泣并且责备?
啊,我的兄弟们,你还宣讲什么教义?
因为说上帝存在对于这二者都很怀疑。

十二

让孩子们就在你面前哭泣吧,
他们在跑步以前便精疲力尽。
他们从没见过阳光,也没见过光荣,
据说这比太阳还要光明。
他们懂得人类的悲哀,却不懂智慧。

他们沉没在人类的绝望中,得不到安静。
他们是奴隶,毫无基督世界的自由自在,
是殉道者,没有奖赏,只有剧痛,
衰弱了,仿佛上了年纪,而无法弥补,
不能留下半点亲切的记忆,
是尘世和天堂之爱的弃孤:
让他们哭泣吧!让他们哭泣!

十三

他们仰起苍白瘦削的脸,
他们的神色令人震惊!
因为他们使你想起无所不在的天使,
生就一双只有天神才会具有的眼睛。
"还要多久,"他们说,"多久,啊,残忍的国度,
你要多久踩在一个孩子的心上来推动世界,
用钉上铁掌的靴跟使心跳窒息住,
就在市场中一路踩着走向你的王位?
我们的血往上喷,啊,我们的暴君,
而你的紫袍[①]显耀了你的前程,
然而孩子们在沉默中的呜咽,
却比一个强壮的人在愤怒中诅咒得更深!"

---

① 紫袍系指帝王之袍。

The Cry of the Children

Do ye hear the children weeping, O my brothers,
Ere the sorrow comes with years?
They are leaning their young heads against their mothers,
And that cannot stop their tears.
The young lambs are bleating in the meadows,
The young birds are chirping in the nest,
The young fawns are playing with the shadows,
The young flowers are blowing toward the west:
But the young, young children, O my brothers,
They are weeping bitterly!
They are weeping in the playtime of the others,
In the country of the free.

Do you question the young children in the sorrow,
Why their tears are falling so?
The old man may weep for his to-morrow
Which is lost in Long Ago;
The old tree is leafless in the forest,
The old year is ending in the frost,
The old wound, if stricken, is the sorest,
The old hope is hardest to be lost.
But the young, young children, O my brothers,
Do you ask them why they stand
Weeping sore before the bosoms of their mothers,
In our happy Fatherland?

They look up with their pale and sunken faces,
And their looks are sad to see,
For the man's hoary anguish draws and presses

Down the cheeks of infancy.
"Your old earth," they say, "is very dreary;"
"Our young feet," they say, "are very weak;
Few paces have we taken, yet are weary—
Our grave-rest is very far to seek:
Ask the old why they weep, and not the children,
For the outside earth is cold,
And we young ones stand without, in our bewildering,
And the graves are for the old."

"True," say the children, "it may happen
That we die before our time:
Little Alice died last year, her grave is shapen
Like a snowball, in the rime.
We looked into the pit prepared to take her:
Was no room for any work in the close clay!
From the sleep wherein she lieth none will wake her,
Crying, 'Get up, little Alice! it is day.'
If you listen by that grave, in sun and shower,
With your ear down, little Alice never cries:
Could we see her face, be sure we should not know her,
For the smile has time for growing in her eyes:
And merry go her moments, lulled and stilled in
The shroud, by the kirk-chime.
It is good when it happens," say the children,
"That we die before our time."

Alas, alas the children! they are seeking
Death in life, as best to have;
They are binding up their hearts away from breaking,
With a cerement from the grave.
Go out, children, from the mine and from the city,
Sing out, children, as the little thrushes do;

Pluck you handfuls of the meadow-cowslips pretty,
Laugh aloud, to feel your fingers let them through!
But they answer, "Are your cowslips of the meadows
Like our weeds anear the mine?
Leave us quiet in the dark of the coal-shadows,
From your pleasures fair and fine!

"For oh," say the children, "we are weary,
And we cannot run or leap;
If we cared for any meadows, it were merely
To drop down in them and sleep.
Our knees tremble sorely in the stooping,
We fall upon our faces, trying to go;
And, underneath our heavy eyelids drooping,
The reddest flower would look as pale as snow.
For, all day, we drag our burden tiring
Through the coal-dark, underground,
Or, all day, we drive the wheels of iron
In the factories, round and round.

"For all day, the wheels are droning, turning;
Their wind comes in our faces,
Till our hearts turn, our heads, with pulses burning,
And the walls turn in their places:
Turns the sky in the high window blank and reeling,
Turns the long light that drops adown the wall,
Turn the black flies that crawl along the ceiling,
All are turning, all the day, and we with all.
And all day, the iron wheels are droning;
And sometimes we could pray,
'O ye wheels,' (breaking out in a mad moaning)
'Stop! be silent for to-day!'"

Ay, be silent! Let them hear each other breathing
For a moment, mouth to mouth!
Let them touch each other's hands, in a fresh wreathing
Of their tender human youth!
Let them feel that this cold metallic motion
Is not all the life God fashions or reveals:
Let them prove their inward souls against the notion
That they live in you, or under you, O wheels!
Still, all day, the iron wheels go onward,
Grinding life down from its mark;
And the children's souls, which God is calling sunward,
Spin on blindly in the dark.

Now tell the poor young children, O my brothers,
To look up to Him and pray;
So the blessed One who blesseth all the others,
Will bless them another day.
They answer, "Who is God that He should hear us,
While the rushing of the iron wheels is stirred?
When we sob aloud, the human creatures near us
Pass by, hearing not, or answer not a word.
And we hear not (for the wheels in their resounding)
Strangers speaking at the door.
Is it likely God, with angels singing round Him,
Hears our weeping any more?

"Two words, indeed, of praying we remember,
And at midnight's hour of harm,
'Our Father,' looking upward in the chamber,
We say softly for a charm.
We know no other words, except 'Our Father,'
And we think that, in some pause of angels' song,
God may pluck them with the silence sweet to gather,

And hold both within His right hand which is strong.
'Our Father!' If He heard us, He would surely
(For they call Him good and mild)
Answer, smiling down the steep world very purely,
'Come and rest with me, my child.

"But, no!" say the children, weeping faster,
"He is speechless as a stone:
And they tell us, of His image is the master
Who commands us to work on.
Go to!" say the children,--"up in Heaven,
Dark, wheel-like, turning clouds are all we find.
Do not mock us; grief has made us unbelieving:
We look up for God, but tears have made us blind."
Do you hear the children weeping and disproving,
O my brothers, what ye preach?
For God's possible is taught by His world's loving,
And the children doubt of each.

And well may the children weep before you!
They are weary ere they run:
They have never seen the sunshine, nor the glory,
Which is brighter than the sun.
They know the grief of man, without its wisdom.
They sink in the despair, without its calm:
Are slaves, without the liberty in Christdom,
Are martyrs, by the pang without the palm:
Are worn as if with age, yet unretrievingly
The harvest of its memories cannot reap,—
Are orphans of the earthly love and heavenly.
Let them weep! let them weep!

They look up, with their pale and sunken faces,

And their look is dread to see,
For they think you see their angels in high places,
With eyes turned on Deity.
"How long," they say, "how long, O cruel nation,
Will you stand, to move the world, on a child's heart,—
Stifle down with a mailed heel its palpitation,
And tread onward to your throne amid the mart?
Our blood splashes upward, O gold-heaper,
And your purple shows your path!
But the child's sob in the silence curses deeper
Than the strong man in his wrath."

伊丽莎白·巴莱特·勃朗宁 / 作
Elizabeth Barrett Browning. 1806—1861
杨苡 / 译

在西班牙被炸死的儿童

蜡偶的脸更红,可是这些是小孩子。
他们眼睛不是玻璃,是闪光的纤维。
黑的眸子,在那水银一般的顾盼里,
日光曾颤动过。这些灰白色的嘴唇
曾经是温暖的,而有过灿烂的血色,
可是那时的血
是藏在湿润的皮肤里,
而不是纷溅在乱发上。

在这些黑发中间,
红色的花不常是
如此凝成了黑块。

这些是死了的脸,
蜂巢也不更惨淡,
木烬也不更灰白。

他们被列成一行,
如落地的纸灯笼,
经过一夜的狂欢,
干燥晨气中湮灭。

Bombing Casualties: Spain

Dolls' faces are rosier but these were children
their eyes not glass but gleaming gristle
dark lenses in whose quick silvery glances
the sunlight quivered. These blenched lips
were warm once and bright with blood
but blood
held in a moist blob of flesh
not spilt and spatter'd in tousled hair.

In these shadowy tresses
red petals did not always
thus clot and blacken to a scar.

These are dead faces:
wasps' nests are not more wanly waxen
wood embers not so grely ashen.

They are laid out in ranks
like paper lanterns that have fallen
after a night of riot
extinct in the dry morning air

赫伯特・里德 / 作
Herbert Read, 1893—1968
杨宪益 / 译

你脸上的水

你脸上的水被我螺丝转动
的地方,你的枯干的魂吹着,
死尸露出它的白眼。
冰里的鲛人曾梳他们的发的地方,
只有枯干的风驶过,
在盐卤草根鱼卵间。
你的绿色的缨结曾紧缚着
潮汐里船绳的地方,又来了
那个绿色的解缚者。
他剪上加油,刀松弛地悬着,
来把这水流从它的根切断,
取下潮湿的果实。
不被人注意,你按时的潮汐,
在水草的婚寝上,撞击,流散,
而离开枯干的水草。
在你岩石间,小孩子的阴影
徘徊,而从他们空旷的地方,
向有鲯鳅的海呼叫。
虽如海一般干,但斑斓的匣盖
当不加锁,只要圣美的魔力
还在天地中间徜徉。
应当还有珊瑚在你的水底,
应当还有蛟龙在你潮汐里,
除非失去海的信仰。

Where Once The Waters Of Your Face

Where once the waters of your face
Spun to my screws, your dry ghost blows,
The dead turns up its eye;
Where once the mermen through your ice
Pushed up their hair, the dry wind steers
Through salt and root and roe.

Where once your green knots sank their splice
Into the tided cord, there goes
The green unraveller,
His scissors oiled, his knife hung loose
To cut the channels at their source
And lay the wet fruits low.

Invisible, your clocking tides
Break on the lovebeds of the weed;
The weed of love's left dry;
There round about your stone the shades
Of children go who, from their voids,
Cry to the dolphined sea.

Dry as a tomb, your coloured lids
Shall not be latched while magic glides
Sage on the earth and sky;
There shall be corals in your beds
There shall be serpents in your tides,
Till all our sea-faiths die.

迪伦·托马斯 / 作
Dylan Thomas, 1914—1953
杨宪益 / 译

我的愿望

我的愿望是走进那间屋子,
意识的最后一间顶阁。那是
在那过道最后转弯的后面。
我写作时,字句诗辞是钥匙,
爱也是办法,不过不大可靠。
里面有火,我想,最后有真理,
深藏在木柜里,有时我走近,
可是风吹灭火柴,我迷了路。
有时我运气好,找着了钥匙,
把门开了一两寸,可是总有
门铃响,有人叫,或人喊失火,
使我手停住,什么也看不见,
我又跑下楼来,而重新懊悔。

(英文版本未找到)

约翰·莱曼 / 作
John Lehman, 1907—1987
杨宪益 / 译

将死者的歌

什么丧钟,为这些如牛羊的人?
只有大炮的非常巨大的震怒,
只有得得的步枪的响声急速,
能为他们匆忙地奏一曲招魂。
他们没有祈祷,或丧钟的嘲笑,
没有哀泣声音,只有这大合唱!
枪弹惨厉尖锐疯狂的大合唱!
和悲哀的家园,招魂时的号角。
在那里有送死者安眠的明烛?
不在小儿手中。他们自己眼里,
将有永别的圣洁的光辉燃起。
少女额上苍白,将是他们罩布。
寂寂心里的温馨,是他们的花,
和每天黄昏时,窗幕低低垂下。

Anthem for Doomed Youth

What passing-bells for these who die as cattle?
— Only the monstrous anger of the guns.
Only the stuttering rifles' rapid rattle
Can patter out their hasty orisons.
No mockeries now for them; no prayers nor bells;
Nor any voice of mourning save the choirs,—
The shrill, demented choirs of wailing shells;
And bugles calling for them from sad shires.

What candles may be held to speed them all?
Not in the hands of boys, but in their eyes
Shall shine the holy glimmers of goodbyes.
The pallor of girls' brows shall be their pall;
Their flowers the tenderness of patient minds,
And each slow dusk a drawing-down of blinds.

威尔弗雷德·欧文 / 作
Wilfred Owen, 1893—1918
杨宪益 / 译

一个死在战争里的人

比标准时间晚五点钟,
铁鹭来过,又遁去无踪。
荒淫的城,同它的琐碎,很快的烧尽。圣诞树没有
圣灵,无用的树。
他生地是一南方小城,
在白垩的山边睡沉沉。
只是在远处才能看见的白垩的马,还是扬起右蹄。
石里的海绵,早已成了灰。
他们常常说,这个少年
如运气好,能走得很远。
运气是菩提树同梨树开着谢着的花。运气是数着花蕊,
是鸟翼的闪光,是一红球滚过一大片平地,落到
乌有的囊里,可是同时也有奈河,一条宽广的水,
在那里事业终了。
二十三岁,在寂寂世间,
他还未偿了他的夙愿。
因人生起处虽宽,但越升高越险窄,在山顶,祭师持着刀。
奇怪,夜晚十点钟是这里早晨三点钟。
在美洲永不觉得的五点钟里,祭师卷起他的袖子。
我们还没有上床睡觉,
他已睡着,他已经死了。
也没有鼓声,也没有雷声,只有粉笔在黑板上发出细响。
一地积雪里的一片雪花,空白与等号间的零。一本无人
再打开的书里的一朵压起的花。

(英文版本未找到)

路易斯·麦克尼斯 / 作
Louis MacNeice, 1907—1963

杨宪益 / 译

送葬

死只是他们路上的界石,
笑在唇边,风在他们四围,
他们只说
他做机器皮带胜过别人。

这是欢乐,是统计的时间,
他们记录一单位的贡献。
他们高兴地送他入土去,
感谢他留给他们的成绩。

走回家想着飘扬的红旗,
欢歌的旗也在血里摇曳,
他们梦想着大同的世界,
城市如神经中枢和动脉。

也想起人生,营营劳动着,
如金色歌咏的轮中一齿,
如火花溅出,完成了工作,
寂寂地落去。

他们不为个人感觉悲哀,
没有大人物虚伪的眼泪,
不同学究们,梦想古希腊的魂灵,
为时代衰亡忧泣。

(英文版本未找到)

斯蒂芬·史彭德 / 作
Stephen Spender, 1909—1995

杨宪益 / 译

升天节

这难道是件神圣的事情,
在一个富饶的地方,
婴儿们干瘦得十分凄惨,
竟让那冰冷的放债的手来喂养?

那颤抖的叫声可算是支歌?
它难道能是一曲欢快的歌曲?
还有那么多的穷苦孩子?
那原来是个穷瘠的地方!

他们的太阳永远不会发光。
他们的田野是光秃秃的一片荒原。
他们的道路荆棘丛生,
那里就是永无止境的冬天。

因为只要哪里有阳光照耀,
只要哪里会降下甘霖,
婴儿就不会在那里挨饿,
贫穷也不会威吓着心灵。

Holy Thursday

Is this a holy thing to see
In a rich and fruitful land.
Babes reduced to misery.
Fed with cold and usurous hand?

Is that trembling cry a song?
Can it be a song of joy?
And so many children poor?
It is a land of poverty!

And their sun does never shine.
And their fields are bleak & bare.
And their ways are fill'd with thorns
It is eternal winter there.

For where-e'er the sun does shine.
And where-e'er the rain does fall:
Babe can never hunger there,
Nor poverty the mind appall.

威廉·布莱克 / 作
William Blake, 1757—1827
杨苡 / 译

咏希朗十四行诗

无束缚的心境的永生之灵!
自由!你在地牢中是最辉煌的,
因为你居住在人们的心里——
只有对你的热爱才能联起这些心;
当你的子孙被戴上枷锁——
和那潮湿地窖的不见天日的幽暗,
他们的国家战胜了,由于他们的殉难,
自由的荣誉随着阵风而传播。
希朗!你的监狱是一块圣地,
你的阴惨的地板是祭坛——
因为邦尼瓦来回踱着竟使他的脚步每下痕迹,
仿佛你这冰冷的石板
是草地!让那些痕迹不要消减!
为了它们在暴政下向神的求援!

Sonnet on Chillon

Eternal Spirit of the chainless Mind!
Brightest in dungeons, Liberty! thou art,
For there thy habitation is the heart—
The heart which love of thee alone can bind;
And when thy sons to fetters are consign'd—
To fetters, and the damp vault's dayless gloom,
Their country conquers with their martyrdom,
And freedom's fame finds wings on every wind.
Chillon! thy prison is a holy place,
And thy sad floor an altar—for t'was trod,
Until his very steps have left a trace
Worn, as if thy cold pavement were a sod,
By Bonnivard! May none those marks efface!
For they appeal from tyranny to God

乔治·戈登·拜伦 / 作
George Gordon Byron, 1788—1824
杨苡 / 译

希朗的囚徒

我的头发灰白了,非由于年迈,
也不是仅仅在一夜里
就忽然变成白的,
正像人们出于骤然的惊骇!
我的四肢弯曲了,不是由于劳累,
却由于一种卑鄙的休息而废弃,
因为它被地牢的摧毁,
我的命运和那些人是一样的。
对于他们,大地和空气
是禁止的,向往的——全被隔离;
但这是为了我父亲的信仰,
我忍受了锁链并且招惹来死亡;
父亲葬身在火刑里,
为了他的不能背弃的主义;
同样的原因使他的后代,
在黑暗中找到了栖身的所在;
我们是七人——现在只有一人,
六个正年轻,一个已衰老,
刚刚开始就结束了生命,
骄傲于迫害的狂暴;
一个死在火里,两个死在战地,
热血给他们的信仰施以洗礼,
像他们的父亲一样地死去,
为了他们的敌人所否认的正义;
被丢在地牢中的是三个人,

如今只剩下一个孤零了。

那里有七根哥特式的房栋,
架在希朗的深深的古老的地牢中,
那里有七根笨重的灰色的柱,
由于狱中阴暗的光线而变得模糊,
它穿过那倒塌的厚墙上的
裂缝和缝而离去;
像一盏沼泽上的闪烁的灯
爬过如此潮湿的地层;
每一根房栋有一个环,
每一个环上套一条锁链;
那铁器是一种使人溃烂的东西,
因为在四肢上还留着它咬的痕迹,
带着不会消失的创痕,
直到万事休了的新时辰,
现在只是使我的眼睛痛苦,
它有多少年不曾见过太阳升出——
我已不能将时日细数,
我失去那冗长繁重的纪录,
当我最后的弟弟倒下死去,
我躺在他身旁尚有气息。

他们把我们每人锁在一石柱,
我们是三个人——但每人是单独;
我们一步也不能动,
我们不能看见彼此的面孔,
在那黯淡的铅色的光辉中,

在我们的眼里竟使我们变成陌生人；
如此长在一起——却是分离，
手虽被铐住，心灵却相联系，
那仍然是一种慰藉，
在这缺乏纯真成分的大地里，
谛听彼此的诉说，
互相要变成安慰者，
凭着一些新的希望或古老的传说，
或者一些豪放的英雄的歌；
然而即或亮些终于也要冷落。
我们的嗓音也变得沉闷，
成了地牢中石头的回声，
一种刺耳的声音，不饱满不奔放，
在往昔绝不愿使它这样；
那也许是幻想，但是我想
它绝不像是我们自己的声音。

我是三人中的大哥，
我要勉强鼓舞其余的人，
我应该这样做——并且尽我所能
他们每人也尽力做得不错。
最小的，为我父亲所宠爱，
因为他继承了我母亲的容颜，
眼睛蓝得像青天——
为了他，我的灵魂痛苦的激动；
的确会使人悲戚，
眼看着这样一个鸟儿在这样一个窝里；
因为他像白昼一样的美丽——

（当白书对于我还很美丽的
正如对幼鹰一样，当他是自由的）——
一个雨季的日子，看不见日落，
直到它的夏季逝去，
那漫长光辉里的不寐的夏令，
太阳的被雪覆盖的后裔；
他就是这样的纯洁和欢欣，
在他愉快的天性里，
流泪只是为了别人的苦难，
然后泪水就流下一如山川，
除非他能够减轻
他所厌恶看到的不幸。

另一个有着同样纯洁的心，
却生成和他的同类竞争；
强壮的体魄，有着
一种和世界敌对的气质，
带着欢乐在最前列中毁灭；
却不是在锁链里憔悴
他的精神在锁链的银铛声中萎谢，
我看它默默的衰颓——
或者事实上我也如此衰颓；
然而我还是竭力使他们欢欣，
这么亲密的一家剩余的人。
他是群山中的一个猎人，
在那里他曾追逐过鹿和狼群；
对于他，他的地牢是个深坑，
锁住的脚是最糟糕的不幸。

莱蒙湖躺在希朗的墙旁；
大量的河流汇聚并流动，
水下面有一千尺深；
这样从希朗的雪白的城堞，
放出许许多多的测量锤，
四通澎湃着海的波浪；
墙与浪造成了双重的牢狱——
像是一个活生生的坟墓，
在那湖水的下面
就是我们置身的黑暗的拱形牢临界，
日日夜夜我们听见微波涟漪；
听着是在我们头顶上的冲撞；
我感觉冬天的浪烟
冲洗着栅栏，当猛烈的风
恣戏在欢乐的天空；
于是这块岩石就在摇荡，
或感到它摇动，却不胆丧，
因为我就能微笑着欢迎
那可以使我自由的死神。

我说过我的亲兄弟已憔悴，
我说他伟大的精神在衰颓。
他厌恶并且把他的三餐推开了；
并且不是由于那太粗糙，
因为我们曾习惯了猎人的食物，
对这些事并不怎么在乎；
从山中羊群挤下的奶
变成从壕井中流出的水，

我们的面包仿佛被囚徒们的眼泪
浸湿了几千个年岁,
自从人开始将他的同类禁闭,
一如将野兽关在铁笼里;
但是这些对我们或对他又有什么关系;
这些伤害不了他的心或身体;
我弟弟的灵魂是那一种典型,
就是在一座宫殿里也会变冷,
如果他自由的呼吸
被峻岭旁的山脉所隔离;
但是为什么拖延这桩事实?——他已死了。
我眼看着,无法将他的头扶起,
无法碰到他僵硬的手——也无法死,
虽然我苦苦的挣扎,却挣扎徒然,
总不能将我的绳索撕开咬成两段。
他死了,他们解下他的锁链,
给他挖了一个浅浅的墓,
就是用我们牢洞里冰冷的土,
我恳求他们赐一个恩典,
把他的尸体埋在白日能照着的尘埃里面——
那是一个愚蠢的思想,
然而在我的脑海中确如此盼望,
因为即或他死去了,他的奔放的心胸
绝不能憩息在这样的一个地牢中。
我或者会吝惜我无用的请愿——
他们冷酷的笑了,仍把他放在那边;
那平坦的无草的土地将他覆盖——
那个人我们是如此的热爱;

上面放着他的锁链已然作废,
那正是对这类谋杀最合适的墓碑!

而他,这个至宝,这朵花,
自从他出生,我们最珍爱他,
美丽的脸上有着他母亲的面影,
他的整个家族的赤子的爱情,
他殉身的父亲最宝贵的思念,
我最后的关注,为了他我甘愿
尽我一生使他的生命现在少吃苦头,
而且总有天获得自由;
他也曾不倦的保持
一种天生的或启发的意志——
他也是被打击了,一天天的
他渐渐在枝头上失去生气。
哦,上帝!那真是一件可怕的事,
眼看着人类的灵魂插翅飞去,
以任何种形态,任何种方式;
我见过它从血泊中一冲而出,
我见过它在波涛冲击的海洋上
以汹涌的震撼天地的行动来顽抗,
我见过那罪恶的憎恶的床,
由于恐惧发着吒狂;
但那些是恐怖——这是悲惨,
并且不与那些相混——却是平稳和缓慢;
他凋谢了,这么宁静又温和,
这么轻轻的消损,这么甜蜜的软弱,
这样的无泪,却又这样深情,仁爱,

并且为那些他撇下的人们而悲哀；
始终有着一张鲜艳的面颊，
仿佛是来自坟墓的一个嘲骂，
它的色泽柔和地消减，
像一道将离去的彩虹的光线；
眼睛有着最清澈的光，
简直把这座地牢照亮，
没吐出一个字的埋怨，
对于他的不逢时的命运也没有一声叹息——
或者谈一些较美好的时光，
一点能鼓舞我自己的希望，
因为我沉在沉默里——迷失了自己，
为了这最后的损失，也是最大的；
他还要压抑，
那衰微的体力软弱的喘息，
逐渐缓慢，渐渐减低；
我静听，却听不见；
我叫喊，因为我吓得疯癫；
我知道是无望了，但是我的恐怖
并且不能如此止住；
我叫喊，我想我听到一个声音——
我使劲一跳，挣开我的锁链，
向他冲去——我找不到他在哪里，
只有我活动在这块黝黑的土地，
只有我活着，只有我呼吸
这潮湿地牢的可诅咒的气息；
这最后的，唯一的，最亲爱的一环
在我和那永生的边缘之间，

它曾使我和我的惨败的家族相连，
却在这命中注定的地方割断。
一边在地上，一边在地底——
我的弟弟们——全停止了呼吸；
我拿起那只手，它摆得这么平稳，
天啊！我自由的手却是同样的冰冷；
我没有力量再奋起或斗争，
可是觉得我还是在一种狂乱的感觉，当我们知道
我们所爱好的将永不能爱好。
我不知道何故
我竟不能死去，
我没有世俗的希望——只有信仰，
就是它禁止一个自私的死亡。

当时在那儿我又遭遇了什么，
我不太知道——我永远不能判断——
起初丧失了光和空气，
后来也失去了黑暗；
我没有思想，没有感觉——什么都没有——
在这些石头当中我站着也像块石头，
我究竟知道什么，简直不能意识，
正像是浓雾中的峻岭没有树枝；
因为一切是空白，荒凉而又黯淡；
那不是夜晚，那不是白天；
甚至也不是这地牢的光亮，
这样憎厌的对着我沉重的目光，
却是空间充塞着空虚，
而且凝固得没有一点位置，

没有星星，没有大地，没有时刻，
没有计算，没有变化，没有至善，没有罪恶，
只有沉寂，和毫无动静的气息，
不是有生命的，也不是死的；
是一泓停滞的死水，
没有出路，无边，缄默，而且静止！

在我的头脑里闪进一道光彩——
那是一只鸟的讴歌；
它停住了，然后又重来，
那里最甜蜜的歌唱从未听过，
我的耳朵充满了感谢，当我的眼睛
惊喜地滑过这般情景，
那一瞬间他们看不出
我是苦难的伴侣；
但是以后慢慢地，我的理性
回到它们习惯的路程；
我看见这地牢的墙和地板
紧紧把我包围一如以前，
我看见太阳的光芒
潜行着和过去一样，
但是穿过裂缝那里现出
那只惹人怜爱的驯服的鸟儿栖于椽木，
而且比在树上更显得驯服；
一只可爱的鸟，有着天蓝色的翅
还有诉说着千万件事的歌子，
而且一切像为我而吐诉！
我以前从未看过这样的事情，

我将永不会再看见什么事与这相近；
它仿佛像我一样渴求一个知己，
但是它却没有我一半的孤寂，
它是来爱我的，当爱我的人
再没有一个生存，
从我地牢边缘来使我欢畅，
使我又重新能感觉能思想。
我不知道它是否才获得自由，
或者啄开它的笼子栖在我这里，
但是我太深知被囚禁的哀愁，
甜蜜的鸟！我不能愿望它给你！
也许是它披了翅膀来乔装，
从天堂下降来造访，
因为——上帝原谅我这个思想，这时
使我又要微笑，又要哭泣——
我有时竟以为也许是，
我弟弟的魂灵下凡到我这里；
然而终于它还是飞开，
我这才知道这仍是人间的形骸，
因为他绝不会这样的死去，
两次撇下我使我加倍的孤寂，
孤寂犹如裹在寿衣里的死人，
孤寂犹如一朵孤零零的云，
晴朗的天气时一朵单独的云，
当天空的一切是那么澄清，
却像是对这气氛一个怒容，
这是不该出现的事情，
当天空是蓝蓝的，大地在欢欣。

我的命运中有了一种改变，
我的狱卒竟对我哀怜；
我不知道是什么使他们如此，
他们早已习于目睹痛苦，
然而真是的：——我破旧的锁链
不再紧扣着那些铁环，
而且可以有自由散步，
从这边到那边沿着我的牢狱，
走来走去，然而再横过，
践踏着差不多每一个角落；
绕过那些柱子，一个个连接，
然后再回到我开始散步的地点，
当我漫步时，只避免步行
到我弟弟们那些没有草皮的坟；
因为我一旦想到不小心的漫步，
我的脚步污渎了他们的床铺，
我的呼吸就会窒息而浊重，
我的碎了的心感到难过而不知。

我的墙上挖了一个放脚的地方，
不是打算从那里逃奔，
因为我已把他们一一埋葬，
他们爱过我当他们还是活人；
从此这整个的大地
对于我就变成一个较宽阔的监狱；
我没有孩子，没有父辈，没有亲属，
也没有伴侣分担我的悲苦；

我想到这里，我还会喜欢，
因为一想到他们就使我疯癫；
然而我还是好奇地攀上
我那些栅栏窗子，
再一次投出爱抚的窥探的目光，
瞭望那些高高的山岭。

我看见它们，它们都还如故，
它们没有改变正像我的心境也还仿佛；
我看见在上面有它们千年的白雪——
下面是它们的宽阔的湖水，
还有那蓝色的隆尼河川流不息；
我听见激流跳跃又汹涌，
越过海湾的岩石和断裂的矮丛；
我看见远处白色墙壁的市镇，
还有更白的帆船斜着划行，
那边还有一个小小的岛，
它正在朝着我微笑，
这是唯一可以看见的；
一个小小的绿岛，看来只是这个
比我的地牢的地板并不宽阔，
然而在那里有三棵高高的树，
山上的微风在树上面吹拂，
它旁边有海水在流动，
它上边有娇嫩的花儿茁生，
有着柔和的颜色和香气。
鱼儿游泳在城堡旁，
它们看来彼此都很欢畅；

苍鹰驾驭着升起的暴风,
我想他从来没有这么迅速的飞行,
如我本来设想的一样;
于是新的眼泪又涌上我的眼眶,
我觉得烦恼——甚至宁愿
我没有脱掉我先前的锁链;
而当我再爬下到地面,
我的阴惨住处的黑暗
落在我头上像个沉重的负担;
它像是一个新掘好的坟,
封闭着一个我们请求赦免的人,——
但是我的目光,为了过多的压抑,
简直需要这样的一种休息。

不知是多少月,多少年,或多少天,
我没有数算,也没有用笔记,
我不希望抬起我的双眼,
清算那些倦人的琐细;
终于人们走来将我释放;
我没问为什么,也不在乎到何去何方,
 "到末了什么对于我都是一样,"
被捆绑或不被捆绑,
我学会了喜爱绝望。
因此当最后他们出现,
并且所有我的桎梏全抛在一边,
这些沉重的墙竟成就
一个隐舍——一切都为我所有!
我都有些觉得他们来

仿佛是把我从第二个家拖开；
我和蜘蛛有过友谊，
眼看着他们在他们惨淡的经营里，
曾看过老鼠在月光下戏耍，
为什么我反要觉得我比它们缺乏？
我们是一个地方的同住者，
我，各个种族的君主，
有权利屠杀——但说来颇惊奇！
我们学会了居住在安静里；
我这份锁链和我变成了相知，
这么一个悠久的交情驱使
我们成一个现在的我们：我甚至就
叹息着重获我的自由。

The Prisoner of Chillon

My hair is grey, but not with years,
Nor grew it white
In a single night,
As men's have grown from sudden fears:
My limbs are bow'd, though not with toil,
But rusted with a vile repose,
For they have been a dungeon's spoil,
And mine has been the fate of those
To whom the goodly earth and air
Are bann'd, and barr'd—forbidden fare;
But this was for my father's faith
I suffer'd chains and courted death;
That father perish'd at the stake
For tenets he would not forsake;
And for the same his lineal race
In darkness found a dwelling place;
We were seven—who now are one,
Six in youth, and one in age,
Finish'd as they had begun,
Proud of Persecution's rage;
One in fire, and two in field,
Their belief with blood have seal'd,
Dying as their father died,
For the God their foes denied;—
Three were in a dungeon cast,
Of whom this wreck is left the last.

There are seven pillars of Gothic mould,
In Chillon's dungeons deep and old,

There are seven columns, massy and grey,
Dim with a dull imprison'd ray,
A sunbeam which hath lost its way,
And through the crevice and the cleft
Of the thick wall is fallen and left;
Creeping o'er the floor so damp,
Like a marsh's meteor lamp:
And in each pillar there is a ring,
And in each ring there is a chain;
That iron is a cankering thing,
For in these limbs its teeth remain,
With marks that will not wear away,
Till I have done with this new day,
Which now is painful to these eyes,
Which have not seen the sun so rise
For years—I cannot count them o'er,
I lost their long and heavy score
When my last brother droop'd and died,
And I lay living by his side.

They chain'd us each to a column stone,
And we were three—yet, each alone;
We could not move a single pace,
We could not see each other's face,
But with that pale and livid light
That made us strangers in our sight:
And thus together—yet apart,
Fetter'd in hand, but join'd in heart,
'Twas still some solace in the dearth
Of the pure elements of earth,
To hearken to each other's speech,
And each turn comforter to each
With some new hope, or legend old,

Or song heroically bold;
But even these at length grew cold.
Our voices took a dreary tone,
An echo of the dungeon stone,
A grating sound, not full and free,
As they of yore were wont to be:
It might be fancy—but to me
They never sounded like our own.

I was the eldest of the three
And to uphold and cheer the rest
I ought to do—and did my best—
And each did well in his degree.
The youngest, whom my father loved,
Because our mother's brow was given
To him, with eyes as blue as heaven—
For him my soul was sorely moved:
And truly might it be distress'd
To see such bird in such a nest;
For he was beautiful as day—
(When day was beautiful to me
As to young eagles, being free)—
A polar day, which will not see
A sunset till its summer's gone,
Its sleepless summer of long light,
The snow-clad offspring of the sun:
And thus he was as pure and bright,
And in his natural spirit gay,
With tears for nought but others' ills,
And then they flow'd like mountain rills,
Unless he could assuage the woe
Which he abhorr'd to view below.

The other was as pure of mind,
But form'd to combat with his kind;
Strong in his frame, and of a mood
Which 'gainst the world in war had stood,
And perish'd in the foremost rank
With joy:—but not in chains to pine:
His spirit wither'd with their clank,
I saw it silently decline—
And so perchance in sooth did mine:
But yet I forced it on to cheer
Those relics of a home so dear.
He was a hunter of the hills,
Had followed there the deer and wolf;
To him this dungeon was a gulf,
And fetter'd feet the worst of ills.

Lake Leman lies by Chillon's walls:
A thousand feet in depth below
Its massy waters meet and flow;
Thus much the fathom-line was sent
From Chillon's snow-white battlement,
Which round about the wave inthralls:
A double dungeon wall and wave
Have made—and like a living grave
Below the surface of the lake
The dark vault lies wherein we lay:
We heard it ripple night and day;
Sounding o'er our heads it knock'd;
And I have felt the winter's spray
Wash through the bars when winds were high
And wanton in the happy sky;
And then the very rock hath rock'd,
And I have felt it shake, unshock'd,

Because I could have smiled to see
The death that would have set me free.

I said my nearer brother pined,
I said his mighty heart declined,
He loathed and put away his food;
It was not that 'twas coarse and rude,
For we were used to hunter's fare,
And for the like had little care:
The milk drawn from the mountain goat
Was changed for water from the moat,
Our bread was such as captives' tears
Have moisten'd many a thousand years,
Since man first pent his fellow men
Like brutes within an iron den;
But what were these to us or him?
These wasted not his heart or limb;
My brother's soul was of that mould
Which in a palace had grown cold,
Had his free breathing been denied
The range of the steep mountain's side;
But why delay the truth?—he died.
I saw, and could not hold his head,
Nor reach his dying hand—nor dead,—
Though hard I strove, but strove in vain,
To rend and gnash my bonds in twain.
He died—and they unlock'd his chain,
And scoop'd for him a shallow grave
Even from the cold earth of our cave.
I begg'd them, as a boon, to lay
His corse in dust whereon the day
Might shine—it was a foolish thought,
But then within my brain it wrought,

That even in death his freeborn breast
In such a dungeon could not rest.
I might have spared my idle prayer—
They coldly laugh'd—and laid him there:
The flat and turfless earth above
The being we so much did love;
His empty chain above it leant,
Such Murder's fitting monument!

But he, the favourite and the flower,
Most cherish'd since his natal hour,
His mother's image in fair face
The infant love of all his race
His martyr'd father's dearest thought,
My latest care, for whom I sought
To hoard my life, that his might be
Less wretched now, and one day free;
He, too, who yet had held untired
A spirit natural or inspired—
He, too, was struck, and day by day
Was wither'd on the stalk away.
Oh, God! it is a fearful thing
To see the human soul take wing
In any shape, in any mood:
I've seen it rushing forth in blood,
I've seen it on the breaking ocean
Strive with a swoln convulsive motion,
I've seen the sick and ghastly bed
Of Sin delirious with its dread:
But these were horrors—this was woe
Unmix'd with such—but sure and slow:
He faded, and so calm and meek,
So softly worn, so sweetly weak,

So tearless, yet so tender—kind,
And grieved for those he left behind;
With all the while a cheek whose bloom
Was as a mockery of the tomb
Whose tints as gently sunk away
As a departing rainbow's ray;
An eye of most transparent light,
That almost made the dungeon bright;
And not a word of murmur—not
A groan o'er his untimely lot,—
A little talk of better days,
A little hope my own to raise,
For I was sunk in silence—lost
In this last loss, of all the most;
And then the sighs he would suppress
Of fainting Nature's feebleness,
More slowly drawn, grew less and less:
I listen'd, but I could not hear;
I call'd, for I was wild with fear;
I knew 'twas hopeless, but my dread
Would not be thus admonishèd;
I call'd, and thought I heard a sound—
I burst my chain with one strong bound,
And rushed to him:—I found him not,
I only stirred in this black spot,
I only lived, I only drew
The accursed breath of dungeon-dew;
The last, the sole, the dearest link
Between me and the eternal brink,
Which bound me to my failing race
Was broken in this fatal place.
One on the earth, and one beneath—
My brothers—both had ceased to breathe:

I took that hand which lay so still,
Alas! my own was full as chill;
I had not strength to stir, or strive,
But felt that I was still alive—
A frantic feeling, when we know
That what we love shall ne'er be so.
I know not why
I could not die,
I had no earthly hope—but faith,
And that forbade a selfish death.

What next befell me then and there
I know not well—I never knew—
First came the loss of light, and air,
And then of darkness too:
I had no thought, no feeling—none—
Among the stones I stood a stone,
And was, scarce conscious what I wist,
As shrubless crags within the mist;
For all was blank, and bleak, and grey;
It was not night—it was not day;
It was not even the dungeon-light,
So hateful to my heavy sight,
But vacancy absorbing space,
And fixedness—without a place;
There were no stars, no earth, no time,
No check, no change, no good, no crime
But silence, and a stirless breath
Which neither was of life nor death;
A sea of stagnant idleness,
Blind, boundless, mute, and motionless!
A light broke in upon my brain,—
It was the carol of a bird;

It ceased, and then it came again,
The sweetest song ear ever heard,
And mine was thankful till my eyes
Ran over with the glad surprise,
And they that moment could not see
I was the mate of misery;
But then by dull degrees came back
My senses to their wonted track;
I saw the dungeon walls and floor
Close slowly round me as before,
I saw the glimmer of the sun
Creeping as it before had done,
But through the crevice where it came
That bird was perch'd, as fond and tame,
And tamer than upon the tree;
A lovely bird, with azure wings,
And song that said a thousand things,
And seemed to say them all for me!
I never saw its like before,
I ne'er shall see its likeness more:
It seem'd like me to want a mate,
But was not half so desolate,
And it was come to love me when
None lived to love me so again,
And cheering from my dungeon's brink,
Had brought me back to feel and think.
I know not if it late were free,
Or broke its cage to perch on mine,
But knowing well captivity,
Sweet bird! I could not wish for thine!
Or if it were, in wingèd guise,
A visitant from Paradise;
For—Heaven forgive that thought! the while

Which made me both to weep and smile—
I sometimes deem'd that it might be
My brother's soul come down to me;
But then at last away it flew,
And then 'twas mortal well I knew,
For he would never thus have flown—
And left me twice so doubly lone,—
Lone as the corse within its shroud,
Lone as a solitary cloud,
A single cloud on a sunny day,
While all the rest of heaven is clear,
A frown upon the atmosphere,
That hath no business to appear
When skies are blue, and earth is gay.

A kind of change came in my fate,
My keepers grew compassionate;
I know not what had made them so,
They were inured to sights of woe,
But so it was:—my broken chain
With links unfasten'd did remain,
And it was liberty to stride
Along my cell from side to side,
And up and down, and then athwart,
And tread it over every part;
And round the pillars one by one,
Returning where my walk begun,
Avoiding only, as I trod,
My brothers' graves without a sod;
For if I thought with heedless tread
My step profaned their lowly bed,
My breath came gaspingly and thick,
And my crush'd heart felt blind and sick.

I made a footing in the wall,
It was not therefrom to escape,
For I had buried one and all,
Who loved me in a human shape;
And the whole earth would henceforth be
A wider prison unto me:
No child, no sire, no kin had I,
No partner in my misery;
I thought of this, and I was glad,
For thought of them had made me mad;
But I was curious to ascend
To my barr'd windows, and to bend
Once more, upon the mountains high,
The quiet of a loving eye.

I saw them—and they were the same,
They were not changed like me in frame;
I saw their thousand years of snow
On high—their wide long lake below,
And the blue Rhone in fullest flow;
I heard the torrents leap and gush
O'er channell'd rock and broken bush;
I saw the white-wall'd distant town,
And whiter sails go skimming down;
And then there was a little isle,
Which in my very face did smile,
The only one in view;
A small green isle, it seem'd no more,
Scarce broader than my dungeon floor,
But in it there were three tall trees,
And o'er it blew the mountain breeze,
And by it there were waters flowing,
And on it there were young flowers growing,

Of gentle breath and hue.
The fish swam by the castle wall,
And they seem'd joyous each and all;
The eagle rode the rising blast,
Methought he never flew so fast
As then to me he seem'd to fly;
And then new tears came in my eye,
And I felt troubled—and would fain
I had not left my recent chain;
And when I did descend again,
The darkness of my dim abode
Fell on me as a heavy load;
It was as is a new-dug grave,
Closing o'er one we sought to save,—
And yet my glance, too much opprest,
Had almost need of such a rest.

It might be months, or years, or days—
I kept no count, I took no note—
I had no hope my eyes to raise,
And clear them of their dreary mote;
At last men came to set me free;
I ask'd not why, and reck'd not where;
It was at length the same to me,
Fetter'd or fetterless to be,
I learn'd to love despair.
And thus when they appear'd at last,
And all my bonds aside were cast,
These heavy walls to me had grown
A hermitage—and all my own!
And half I felt as they were come
To tear me from a second home:
With spiders I had friendship made

And watch'd them in their sullen trade,
Had seen the mice by moonlight play,
And why should I feel less than they?
We were all inmates of one place,
And I, the monarch of each race,
Had power to kill—yet, strange to tell!
In quiet we had learn'd to dwell;
My very chains and I grew friends,
So much a long communion tends
To make us what we are:—even I
Regain'd my freedom with a sigh.

乔治·戈登·拜伦 / 作
George Gordon Byron, 1788—1824
杨苡 / 译

天使

我做了一个梦!怎么说得清?
梦见我竟是个女王,还没有结婚,
被一个温柔的天使护卫,
却并不能排遣我愚蠢的伤悲!

我总是在哭泣,夜晚和白天。
他总是把我的泪水擦干,
我总是在哭泣,白天和夜晚,
我心中的欢悦却向他隐瞒。

因此他就展翅飞走,
清晨抹上玫瑰红的娇羞。
我擦干了眼泪,开始武装,
用一万副盾牌与长矛使我不心慌。

不久我的天使又飞回,
我却已武装戒备,他这是白费。
青春的时光早已不知去向,
我的头上也已白发苍苍。

The Angel

I dreamt a dream! What can it mean?
And that I was a maiden Queen
Guarded by an Angel mild:
Witless woe was ne'er beguiled!

And I wept both night and day,
And he wiped my tears away;
And I wept both day and night,
And hid from him my heart's delight.

So he took his wings, and fled;
Then the morn blushed rosy red.
I dried my tears, and armed my fears
With ten-thousand shields and spears.

Soon my Angel came again;
I was armed, he came in vain;
For the time of youth was fled,
And grey hairs were on my head.

威廉·布莱克 / 作
William Blake, 1757—1827
杨苡 / 译

记忆

记住我吧当我失去的时候,
去到那遥远的寂静的国土。
当你再不能用手将我拖住,
我也不能要走又转来逗留。
记住我当再也不会一天天,
你对我设想着我们的未来。
只是记住我吧,你应该明白,
再劝告祈求也将是太晚。
如若你偶然要忘记我,
过后又想起来也不要难过,
因为若黑暗与腐朽留下我,
曾一度有过的思想的痕迹,
不如你忘记笑笑还好得多,
以免你记起了而后又哀戚。

Remember

Remember me when I am gone away,
Gone far away into the silent land;
When you can no more hold me by the hand,
Nor I half turn to go yet turning stay.
Remember me when no more day by day
You tell me of our future that you plann'd:
Only remember me; you understand
It will be late to counsel then or pray.
Yet if you should forget me for a while
And afterwards remember, do not grieve:
For if the darkness and corruption leave
A vestige of the thoughts that once I had,
Better by far you should forget and smile
Than that you should remember and be sad.

克里斯汀娜·罗塞蒂 / 作
Christina Rossetti, 1830—1894
杨苡 / 译

人生

在绿荫的寂寂的林中,那里我
夏天常去找我爱的寂静,阴影,
我忽然找到外来的死的恫吓,
在树的皱皮上有白漆的痕印。

多少老朋友不能逃脱,现在我
以新的眼光看我城里的旧伴,
也如树一般走着,而每人前额
都有苍白的纹,也都将被砍断。

(英文版本未找到)

杰拉尔德·古尔德 / 作
Gerald Gould, 1885—1936

杨宪益 / 译

辑五

一点,一点,展开在人手上,人能观察宇宙的横切面,用再多一点忍耐和时间。
——《人几乎能够》

夜晚在我周围暗下来

夜晚在我周围暗下来，
狂风冷冷地怒吼，
但有一个蛮横的符咒锁住我，
我不能、不能走。

巨大的树在弯身，
雪压满了它们的枝头。
暴风雪很快降临了，
然而我不能走。

我头上乌云密布，
我下面汪洋奔流。
任什么阴郁也不能使我移动，
我不要，也不能走。

The Night is Darkening Round Me

The night is darkening round me,
The wild winds coldly blow;
But a tyrant spell has bound me,
And I cannot, cannot go.

The giant trees are bending
Their bare boughs weighed with snow;
The storm is fast descending,
And yet I cannot go.

Clouds beyond clouds above me,
Wastes beyond wastes below;
But nothing drear can move me;
I will not, cannot go.

艾米莉·勃朗特 / 作
Emily Brontë, 1818—1848
杨苡 / 译

栗树落下火炬似的繁英

栗树落下火炬似的繁英,
从山楂上,花随着风飞逝,
门关上了,雨使窗上模糊,
给我酒杯,这是暮春时季。

又一春天催短我们生命,
又完了一季被风雨摧毁。
明年的春天也许多晴天,
可是我们将是二十四岁。

我们当然并不是第一个
坐在酒店里,当风雨迅雷
把他们乐观的计划打碎,
咒着创世界的什么坏鬼。

是真的,上天是真不公平,
欺我们有限的一点希冀,
减少我们快乐,当你同我
久劳无功地向坟墓走去。
天不公平,可是给我酒杯,
我们母亲生的不是帝王,
我们所能有的属于凡人。
我们不能要天上的月亮。

如果今天此地雷雨阴阴，
明天阴雨将要远去他处，
旁人躯体将要感觉不快，
旁人心中将要感觉忧郁。

我们骄愤的形骸多忧患，
与永古俱来的，不能没有。
我们忍受，我们必须忍受。
用肩头撑起这阴天，喝酒！

The Chestnut Casts His Flambeaux, and the Flowers

The chestnut casts his flambeaux, and the flowers
Stream from the hawthorn on the wind away,
The doors clap to, the pane is blind with showers.
Pass me the can, lad; there's an end of May.

There's one spoilt spring to scant our mortal lot,
One season ruined of your little store.
May will be fine next year as like as not:
But Ay, but then we shall be twenty-four.

We for a certainty are not the first
Have sat in taverns while the tempest hurled
Their hopeful plans to emptiness, and cursed
Whatever brute and blackguard made the world.

It is in truth iniquity on high
To cheat our sentenced souls of aught they crave,
And mar the merriment as you and I
Fare on our long fool's-errand to the grave.
Iniquity it is; but pass the can.
My lad, no pair of kings our mothers bore;
Our only portion is the estate of man:
We want the moon, but we shall get no more.

If here to-day the cloud of thunder lours
To-morrow it will hie on far behests;
The flesh will grieve on other bones than ours
Soon, and the soul will mourn in other breasts.

The troubles of our proud and angry dust

Are from eternity, and shall not fail.
Bear them we can, and if we can we must.
Shoulder the sky, my lad, and drink your ale.

A. E. 豪斯曼 / 作
A. E. Housman, 1859—1936
杨宪益 / 译

我独自坐着

我独自坐着,夏季的白昼
在微笑的光辉中逝去。
我看见它逝去,我看着它
从迷漫的山丘和无风的草地上消失。

在我的灵魂里思潮进出,
我的心在它的威力下屈从;
在我的眼睛里泪水如涌,
因为我不能把感情说个分明。
就在那个神圣的、无人干扰的时辰,
我四周的严肃的欢悦悄悄溜进。

我问我自己:"啊,上天为什么
不肯把那珍贵的天赋给我,
那光荣的天赋给了许多人,
让他们在诗歌里说出他们的思索!"

"那些梦包围了我,"我说,
"就从无忧虑的童年的欢快时光起。"
狂热的奇想提供出种种的幻想,
自从生命还在它的风华正茂时期。

然而如今,当我曾希望歌唱,
我的手指却触动一根无音的弦,
而歌词的叠句仍然是:
"不要再奋斗了,一切都是枉然。"

Alone I Sat; the Summer Day

Alone I sat; the summer day
Had died in smiling light away;
I saw it die, I watched it fade
From misty hill and breezeless glade;

And thoughts in my soul were gushing,
And my heart bowed beneath their power;
And tears within my eyes were rushing
Because I could not speak the feeling,
The solemn joy around me stealing
In that divine, untroubled hour.

I asked myself, "O why has heaven
Denied the precious gift to me,
The glorious gift to many given
To speak their thoughts in poetry?

"Dreams have encircled me," I said,
"From careless childhood's sunny time;
Visions by ardent fancy fed
Since life was in its morning prime."

But now, when I had hoped to sing,
My fingers strike a tuneless string;
And still the burden of the strain
Is "Strive no more; 'tis all in vain."

艾米莉·勃朗特 / 作
Emily Brontë, 1818—1848
杨苡 / 译

我的心充满了忧愁

我的心充满了忧愁，
为我在往日的知己，
为许多红唇的女儿，
为许多捷足的孩子。

在宽广难涉的河边，
捷足的孩子们安眠，
红唇的女儿们睡在
红蔷薇花谢的田间。

With Rue My Heart is Laden

With rue my heart is laden,
For golden friends I had,
For many a rose-lipt maiden
And many a lightfoot lad.

By brooks too broad for leaping
The lightfoot boys are laid;
The rose-lipt girls are sleeping
In fields where roses fade.

A. E. 豪斯曼 / 作
A. E. Housman, 1859—1936

杨宪益 / 译

我不断地想到

我不断地想到那些真正的英雄
他们生来就记得,灵魂在光辉中的经历,
在那里,时辰光明如太阳,
无尽的歌咏,而他们的可爱的奢望,
就是要用他们仍旧火热的口唇,
述说那自头至踵满了歌诗的灵,
而他们也曾从春枝上采撷藏起,
那如蓓蕾一般缤纷盈袖的相思。

所可宝贵的,就是永远不忘却了,
那在大地未生以前,穿过了石壳,
从古泉源流来血的最初的欢乐。
永远不辞绝薄曙清光中的愉快,
和那在黄昏中肃穆的要求恋爱,
永远不许那俗冗,以雾障和嚣音,
渐渐地遏止了灵的蓓蕾的长成。

在雪旁,日光下,在崇高的田野中,
看那风前的草,是怎么样的尊荣,
以至于那一片片的白色的浮云,
和那寂寂太空中,风的私语同敬
那些人的名字。他们为生命争搏,
他们的心中也曾经藏着光和热,
太阳的后裔,向着太阳暂时迈进,
而已震骇了太空,以他们的灵音。

I Think Continually

I think continually of those who were truly great.
Who, from the womb, remembered the soul's history
Through corridors of light where the hours are suns
Endless and singing. Whose lovely ambition
Was that their lips, still touched with fire,
Should tell of the Spirit clothed from head to foot in song.
And who hoarded from the Spring branches
The desires falling across their bodies like blossoms.

What is precious is never to forget
The essential delight of the blood drawn from ageless springs
Breaking through rocks in worlds before our earth.
Never to deny its pleasure in the morning simple light
Nor its grave evening demand for love.
Never to allow gradually the traffic to smother
With noise and fog the flowering of the spirit.

Near the snow, near the sun, in the highest fields
See how these names are feted by the waving grass
And by the streamers of white cloud
And whispers of wind in the listening sky.
The names of those who in their lives fought for life
Who wore at their hearts the fire's centre.
Born of the sun they travelled a short while towards the sun,
And left the vivid air signed with their honour.

斯蒂芬·史彭德 / 作
Stephen Spender, 1909—1995
杨宪益 / 译

人的抽象观念

那就无须有什么怜悯,
若是我们并没有使人穷困,
也不必再施什么恩德,
若是所有的人都像我们这样快乐。

互相的畏惧带来了和平,
直到自私的爱与日俱增。
于是残酷织成一张罗网,
小心翼翼地把钓饵装上。

他坐下来,怀着神圣的敬畏,
地面沾湿了他的眼泪,
然后谦逊便生了根,
就在他的脚下生存。

不久奥秘在他的头顶,
笼罩阴暗的黑影,
而幼虫和虻蝇,
就靠奥秘喂养为生。

结出了奸诈的果实,
红红的,又甜又好吃,
而乌鸦把他的巢筑成,
就在它那最浓密的树荫。

大地与海洋的诸神,
在大自然中把这棵树遍寻,
但他们的搜寻毫无所得,
在人类的头脑里就长着一棵。

The Human Abstract

Pity would be no more
If we did not make somebody Poor;
And Mercy no more could be
If all were as happy as we.

And mutual fear brings peace,
Till the selfish loves increase:
Then Cruelty knits a snare,
And spreads his baits with care.

He sits down with holy fears,
And waters the grounds with tears;
Then Humility takes its root
Underneath his foot.

Soon spreads the dismal shade
Of Mystery over his head;
And the Caterpillar and Fly
Feed on the Mystery.

And it bears the fruit of Deceit,
Ruddy and sweet to eat;
And the Raven his nest has made
In its thickest shade.

The Gods of the earth and sea
Sought thro' Nature to find this Tree;
But their search was all in vain:
There grows one in the Human Brain.

威廉·布莱克 / 作
William Blake, 1757—1827

杨苡 / 译

为人道主义辩护

悬崖面上黑簇簇的满了爱恋的人。
他们上面的太阳是一袋铁钉。春天的
最初的河流,藏在他们发间。
巨人把手伸入毒井里。
低下头,觉得我的脚,在他脑中走过。
小孩子们追着蝴蝶,转身看见他,
他的手在井里,我的身体从他头中生出,
他们就害怕,丢下捕网,如烟走进墙里。

平滑的原野与它的河流,听着岩石,
如妖蛇吃着花。
小孩子们在圹地的阴影中迷失。
向镜子叫着求救。
"盐的强弓,记忆的弯刀,
写在我的地图上,每一河流的名字。"

一群旗帜奋斗着,出了
叠进的树林,
飞去,如鸟向着炙肉的声响。
沙土落入沸腾的河流里经过望远镜的嘴,
凝成明净的酸滴,带着转舞火焰的花蕊,
纹章的兽,涉过行星的窒息。
蝴蝶从它的皮里挣脱,长出长舌如植物。
植物如云游戏,穿着甲胄。

镜子把巨人的名字写在我前额上,
那时小孩子们已死在圹地的烟里,
爱恋的人如雨从岩上流下。

Salvador Dali

The face of the precipice is black with lovers;
The sun above them is a bag of nails; the spring's
First rivers hide among their hair.
Goliath plunges his hand into the poisoned well
And bows his head and feels my feet walk through his brain.
The children chasing butterflies turn round and see him there
With his hand in the well and my body growing from his head,
And are afraid. They drop their nets and walk into the wall like smoke.

The smooth plain with its mirrors listens to the cliff
Like a basilisk eating flowers.
And the children, lost in the shadows of the catacombs,
Call to the mirrors for help:
'Strong-bow of salt, cutlass of memory,
Write on my map the name of every river.'

A flock of banners fight their way through the telescoped forest
And fly away like birds towards the sound of roasting meat.
Sand falls into the boiling rivers through the telescopes' mouths
And forms clear drops of acid with petals of whirling flame.
Heraldic animals wade through the asphyxia of planets,
Butterflies burst from their skins and grow long tongues like plants,
The plants play games with a suit of mail like a cloud.

Mirrors write Goliath's name upon my forehead,
While the children are killed in the smoke of the catacombs
And lovers float down from the cliffs like rain.

戴维·盖斯科因 / 作
David Gascoyne, 1916—2001
杨宪益 / 译

象征

风雨飘摇的古楼中,
盲目的处士敲着钟。

那无敌的宝刀还是
属于那游荡的傻子。

绣金的锦把宝刀围,
美人同傻子一同睡。

Symbols

A storm-beaten old watch-tower,
A blind hermit rings the hour.

All-destroying sword-blade still
Carried by the wandering fool.

Gold-sewn silk on the sword-blade,
Beauty and fool together laid.

W. B. 叶茨 / 作
W. B. Yeats, 1865—1939

杨宪益 / 译

歌

一年恰逢春季，
一日正在清晨，
早上七点钟整，
山边沾着露珠。
云雀正在展翼，
蜗牛趴在刺丛，
上帝安居天庭——
世界正常有序！

Pippa's Song

The year's at the spring,
And day's at the morn;
Morning's at seven;
The hill-side's dew-pearled;
The lark's on the wing;
The snail's on the thorn;
God's in his Heaven -
All's right with the world!

罗伯特·勃朗宁 / 作
Robert Browning, 1812—1889

杨苡 / 译

序诗

听那行吟诗人的声音!
他看见现在、过去和未来,
他的耳朵听得见,
那神圣的字眼,
漫步在那古老的树林间。

呼唤那堕落的灵魂,
并且在夜晚的露珠中流泪,
也许可以支配
那灿烂的星座
又重新洒下,洒下光辉!

哦,大地!哦,大地醒来!
从露珠沾湿的草地上升。
夜晚已消逝,
而黎明
从那困倦的人群中起身。

不要再转身离去。
你为什么要转身离去?
那星光闪闪照射的地面,
那湿漉漉的海岸,
都给予了你,直至晨曦。

Introduction

Hear the voice of the Bard!
Who present, past, & future, sees;
Whose ears have heard
The Holy Word
That walked among the ancient trees,

Calling the lapsed Soul,
And weeping in the evening dew;
That might controll
The starry pole,
And fallen, fallen light renew!

"O Earth, O Earth, return!
Arise from out the dewy grass;
Night is worn,
And the morn
Rises from the slumbrous mass.

"Turn away no more;
Why wilt thou turn away?
The starry floor,
The wat'ry shore,
Is giv'n thee till the break of day."

威廉·布莱克 / 作
William Blake, 1757—1827
杨苡 / 译

歌

当我死了，我的至爱，
别为我唱悲歌，
别在我头上植玫瑰，
或遮荫的扁柏。
让我上面只有青草，
沾着雨水露滴。
若你愿意，就想念着，
若愿，也可忘记。

我将看不见那阴影，
我将觉不到雨；
我将听不见那夜莺，
唱着像在痛苦；
黄昏时分不再梦想，
不复沉落升起，
也许我还会想念着，
也许便会忘记。

Song

When I am dead, my dearest,
Sing no sad songs for me;
Plant thou no roses at my head,
Nor shady cypress tree:
Be the green grass above me
With showers and dewdrops wet;
And if thou wilt, remember,
And if thou wilt, forget.

I shall not see the shadows,
I shall not feel the rain;
I shall not hear the nightingale
Sing on, as if in pain:
And dreaming through the twilight
That doth not rise nor set,
Haply I may remember,
And haply may forget.

克里斯汀娜·罗塞蒂 / 作
Christina Rossetti, 1830—1894
杨苡 / 译

和声歌辞

命运比任何海窟还幽秘,
当它落在人身上的时候。
春天,仰慕白昼的花出现,
冰崩,白雪从岩石间落下,
使得他离开了他的家园。
没有女人柔手能留住他,
他还是要经过
驿站的守者,丛林的树木,
到异乡的人间,经过大海,
鱼的居处,令人窒息的水。
或孤独在荒原上如野鹑,
在一个多洼穴的石谷中间,
一个在石上盘桓烦恼的鸟。

黄昏时,疲倦,头向前垂下,
梦想到了家园,
窗间的招手,欢迎的陈设,
在大被下吻着他的爱妻。
而醒时只看见
一群无名的鸟,傍人门前
不熟悉的人声,诉说爱恋。

脱离那仇敌设下的罗网,
脱离那道旁猛虎的突袭,
护佑他的家园,

焦念着数着日子的家园，
避免霹雳下击，
避免蔓延如污点的衰灭，
使模糊的日子变为确定，
带来欢乐，和归家的日期，
幸运的日期，将升的曙光。

（英文版本未找到）

W. H. 奥登 / 作
W. H. Auden, 1907—1973

杨宪益 / 译

人几乎能够

你难道不觉得，
你难道不觉得，或者
用更多一点的时间，忍耐
人能把时间的条绪分解。
故意局部地慢慢地欣赏，
分出头绪，分出这样那样，
譬如观察人所践的寸土，
或触一叶一响，己身一部，
不抓住，不碰伤，而要轻轻
用指尖，眼尖，耳尖，不太近，
拿起生命，放在手心当中，
四围温暖，寂寂的不透风，
卧着不动，只轻轻地摇荡，
一点，一点，展开在人手上，
人能观察宇宙的横切面，
用再多一点忍耐和时间。

One Almost Might

Wouldn't you say,
Wouldn't you say: one day,
With a little more time or a little more patience, one might
Disentangle for separate, deliberate, slow delight
One of the moment's hundred strands, unfray
Beginnings from endings, this from that, survey
Say a square inch of the ground one stands on, touch
Part of oneself or a leaf or a sound (not clutch
Or cuff or bruise but touch with finger-tip, ear-
Tip, eyetip, creeping near yet not too near);
Might take up life and lay it on one's palm
And, encircling it in closeness, warmth and calm,
Let it lie still, then stir smooth-softly, and
Tendril by tendril unfold, there on one's hand…

One might examine eternity's cross-section
For a second, with slightly more patience, more time for reflection?

A. S. J. 太息蒙 / 作
A. S. J. Tessimond, 1902—1962

杨宪益 / 译

我是唯一的人

我是唯一的人，命中已注定
无人过问，也无人流泪哀悼
自从我生下来，从未引起过
一线忧虑，一个快乐的微笑。

在秘密的欢乐，秘密的眼泪中，
这变化多端的生活就这样滑过，
度过十八年后仍然无依无靠，
正如在我诞生那天一样的寂寞。

曾有过我躲避不开的时光，
也曾有过那样的时光如此凄凉
当我悲哀的灵魂忘记它的自尊
却渴望这里会有人把我爱上。

然而这只是最初的一闪之念，
此后便被顾虑压倒而缓和，
它们已经逝去了这么久，
现在我难以相信它们曾经有过。

起初青春的希望被融化，
然后幻想的虹彩迅速退开，
于是经验告诉我说真理
决不会在人类的心胸中成长起来。

真够悲哀的是想到人类,
都是不真诚,谄媚和虚伪,
然而更糟的是信赖我自己的心灵,
却发现那儿是一样的颓废。

I Am the Only Being Whose Doom

I am the only being whose doom
No tongue would ask, no eye would mourn;
I never caused a thought of gloom,
A smile of joy, since I was born.

In secret pleasure, secret tears,
This changeful life has slipped away,
As friendless after eighteen years,
As lone as on my natal day.

There have been times I cannot hide,
There have been times when this was drear,
When my sad soul forgot its pride
And longed for one to love me here.

But those were in the early glow
Of feelings since subdued by care;
And they have died so long ago,
I hardly now believe they were.

First melted off the hope of youth,
Then fancy's rainbow fast withdrew;
And then experience told me truth
In mortal bosoms never grew.

'Twas grief enough to think mankind
All hollow, servile, insincere;
But worse to trust to my own mind
And find the same corruption there.

艾米莉·勃朗特 / 作
Emily Brontë, 1818—1848

杨苡 / 译

一个圣像

残酷有一颗人的心,
嫉妒有一张人的脸,
恐怖,披着神圣的人形,
而隐私却穿上了人的衣衫。

人的衣衫,是用铁铸成,
人的外形,是一个炽烈的熔炉。
人的脸,一座封住的炉灶,
人的心,是它饥饿的吞咽之物。

A Divine Image

Cruelty has a Human Heart
And Jealousy a Human Face
Terror the Human Form Divine
And Secrecy, the Human Dress

The Human Dress, is forged Iron
The Human Form, a fiery Forge.
The Human Face, a Furnace seal'd
The Human Heart, its hungry Gorge.

威廉·布莱克 / 作
William Blake, 1757—1827
杨苡 / 译

入睡

人声移动着在这寂静的屋里,
脚步声音,和隐隐关门的余响。
人打着呵欠,只有钟是警醒的。
外面昏暗里,有秋天气息的夜,
充满了窃窃私语的树。在园里,
猎犬空洞的吠声,如空庭铃韵。
我就知道云正移动,掩藏了月,
低而红的初上的月。野鹭叫着,
在它们池边争辩着,磔磔的枭
从林中飞出,在暗淡的麦田上。

等待入睡,我抛开这类的思想,
以今天如梦的事,构造我的梦。
音乐,有一间明亮白色的屋子,
有人唱着一支关于军人的歌,
一两点钟以前,不久这支歌曲
将变为"我梦见他死去",而现在
摇曳的美,经过我脑中。追忆中
旋律的残痕,还能使我的梦境
辉煌,使我看见我曾率领的兵,
数他们的脸,阳光照耀着的脸。
我渐渐入睡了,那些野鹭、猎犬,
昏暗里的九月,和我所熟知的
世界,都渐渐灭去,而进入宁穆。

Falling Asleep

Voices moving about in the quiet house:
Thud of feet and a muffled shutting of doors:
Everyone yawning. Only the clocks are alert.
Out in the night there's autumn-smelling gloom
Crowded with whispering trees; across the park
A hollow cry of hounds like lonely bells:
And I know that the clouds are moving across the moon;
The low, red, rising moon. Now herons call
And wrangle by their pool; and hooting owls
Sail from the wood above pale stooks of oats.

Waiting for sleep, I drift from thoughts like these;
And where to-day was dream-like, build my dreams.
Music ... there was a bright white room below,
And someone singing a song about a soldier,
One hour, two hours ago: and soon the song
Will be 'last night': but now the beauty swings
Across my brain, ghost of remembered chords
Which still can make such radiance in my dream
That I can watch the marching of my soldiers,
And count their faces; faces; sunlit faces.

Falling asleep ... the herons, and the hounds....
September in the darkness; and the world
I've known; all fading past me into peace.

西格弗里德・萨松 / 作
Siegfried Sassoon, 1886—1967
杨宪益 / 译

AGA

睡眠不能带给我欢愉，
记忆永远不会消逝。
我的灵魂已交给苦难，
在叹息中打发日子。

睡眠不能带给我休息，
我清醒着的眼睛永远看不见。
死去的人的影子，
环绕在我的床前。

睡眠不能带给我希望，
他们出现在酣睡之中，
用他们悲哀的形象
使黑暗变得更深更浓。

睡眠不能带给我力量，
没有威力重新鼓起勇气。
我只是在一个更狂暴的海中航行，
在更黑暗的浪涛里。

睡眠不能带给我朋友，
给我安慰和帮忙。
他们熟视无睹，啊，多傲慢！
我只有绝望。

睡眠不能带来愿望,
愈合起我受折磨的心:
我唯一的愿望便是忘记,
在死亡的睡眠之中。

(英文版本未找到)

艾米莉·勃朗特 / 作
Emily Brontë, 1818—1848
杨苡 / 译

墓铭

你应当注意我,我就是"人",
我就是"幸运",我是满足了。
一切我所欲望,比那还多,
我都有了。一切事都顺利。
人生是一假的藏匿地方,
我羞藏,可是被看见讥笑。
再不被人看,不再做傻子,
我知道智慧不敢知的事;
因我知"无有",再不做奴隶,
我解放了自由与无量的
宝藏,因为我得到了"无有"。
我曾追求"美",曾希冀"安息",
现在我得到了"至善"。我是
"至善",我是"无有",我是死了。

Epitaph

ir, you shall notice me: I am the Man;
I am Good Fortune: I am satisfied.
All I desired, more than I could desire,
I have: everything has gone right with me.
Life was a hiding-place that played me false;
I croucht ashamed, and still was seen and scorned:
But now I am not seen. I was a fool,
And now I know what wisdom dare not know:
For I know Nothing. I was a slave, and now
I have ungoverned freedom and the wealth
That cannot be conceived: for I have Nothing.
I lookt for beauty and I longed for rest,
And now I have perfection: nay, I am
perfection: I am nothing, I am dead.

拉塞尔斯·艾伯克龙比 / 作
Lascelles Abercrombie, 1881—1938
杨宪益 / 译

给得撒

无论是什么诞生于肉身，
就必然被尘世消磨殆尽，
为了要摆脱传宗接代的羁绊，
那么我与你有什么相干？

两性从羞耻与骄傲中跃起，
在早晨传播；在夜晚死去，
但慈悲把死亡变成睡眠，
两性激动且哭泣。

你这与我血肉相连的母亲，
用残酷铸造我的心。
用虚假的自欺的泪珠，
把我的鼻孔、眼睛和耳朵束缚。

用没知觉的泥巴使我噤声，
把我出卖给必死的生命：
耶稣的死使我脱离了苦难，
那么我与你有什么相干？

复活的是灵性的身体。

To Tirzah

Whate'er is born of mortal birth
Must be consumèd with the earth,
To rise from generation free:
Then what have I to do with thee?

The sexes sprung from shame and pride,
Blowed in the morn, in evening died;
But mercy changed death into sleep;
The sexes rose to work and weep.

Thou, mother of my mortal part,
With cruelty didst mould my heart,
And with false self-deceiving tears
Didst bind my nostrils, eyes, and ears,

Didst close my tongue in senseless clay,
And me to mortal life betray.
The death of Jesus set me free:
Then what have I to do with thee?

威廉·布莱克 / 作
William Blake, 1757—1827

杨苡 / 译

后记

我已活到103岁这个年纪，好像命运不停地用一把一把苦味的甘果向我掷来，嘲笑我们反抗，却不能说痛！我悄悄地走过这哗笑的人群，静悄悄地独自在一堆堆的烂纸堆中翻弄着，像一个不停地犯错误的小学生，我问自己："这值得吗？"

苦涩的岁月滑过去了，它浸透了我的却不是泪水的回忆，它摆弄着这些烂纸，轻轻说，抚慰着："难道你们这做法不值得一笑吗？"至少对于我们兄妹是有趣的！那些年那些闲言碎语喊喳喳！什么"沉渣泛起""旧瓶装新酒"……让我们钻进故纸堆中吧！我哥对我苦笑着："翻译工作也是一个玩法，人家瞧不起，咱们要挖出它的魅力，很有意思，随便人家去说吧！"用咱们国家的文字给读者换个新鲜的口味。

于是我和我哥在"天亮了"的时候，兴冲冲地说，"咱们是专业中外文学翻译者"，过了几十年风风雨雨，我哥在外文局领导下创办了一个小组——翻译组。

给咱们国家尽可能做一点贡献吧！尽管我们兄妹的能力水平是有限的，我哥和我却始终忠于我们所致力的事业，因为我们的国家已经能做到国泰民安，我们能理解 Peace first！毕竟我们的路已经走尽了一个世纪，尽管走得东歪西倒。

"春去秋来，岁月流逝。游子伤漂泊！回忆儿时、欢声笑语，情景宛如昨……"（忆起一首老歌）

听见我哥低沉的声音："这只是一种尝试，翻译的滋味是有点苦涩，但毕竟……"很有意思！尤其是译诗。

学着不停的咀嚼着一行行诗句,我仿佛又听见我哥笑着说:"咱们译诗是一种文字交流的玩法。"

这真是一种奇妙的文字游戏,它使你夜不能眠。但最后你尝到它的甜味。

我们需要互相说,我们需要友谊,我们能够彼此欣赏,互相尊敬。

Peace! Peace! Peace first!

杨苡

写于多灾多难的 2022 年 3 月

杨苡在写后记,2022 年 3 月

图书在版编目(CIP)数据

杨宪益杨苡兄妹译诗:汉文、英文 / 杨宪益,杨苡译著,赵蘅绘. — 北京:中译出版社,2022.6(2023.2重印)
ISBN 978-7-5001-7069-3

Ⅰ.①杨… Ⅱ.①杨…②杨… Ⅲ.①诗集-世界-汉、英 Ⅳ.①I12

中国版本图书馆CIP数据核字(2022)第080119号

出版发行:中译出版社	
地　　址:北京市西城区新街口外大街28号普天德胜大厦主楼4层	
电　　话:(010)68359827,68359303(发行部);68359725(编辑部)	
传　　真:(010)68357870	邮　　编:100044
电子邮箱:book@ctph.com.cn	网　　址:http://www.ctph.com.cn
出 版 人:乔卫兵	总 策 划:刘永淳
策划编辑:范祥镇　刘瑞莲	责任编辑:刘瑞莲
文字编辑:杨佳特	营销编辑:吴雪峰　董思嫄
封面设计:文件帮	排　　版:文件帮
印　　刷:北京中科印刷有限公司	经　　销:新华书店
规　　格:880 mm×1230 mm	1/32
字　　数:100千字	印　　张:8.125
版　　次:2022年6月第1版	印　　次:2023年2月第2次
ISBN 978-7-5001-7069-3	定　　价:66.00元

本书中10余首诗未找到英文版本,欢迎读者提供线索。

版权所有　侵权必究
中 译 出 版 社